Book One: Be Careful What You Wish For series

# THE WAY OUT

A Novel

Gordon Jensen
with
Cara Highsmith
and
Gordon Thomas

Cara Highsmith
Highsmith Creative Services
cara@highsmithcreative.com



Editing by Cara Highsmith, Highsmith Creative Services, www.highsmithcreative.com
Cover and Interior Design by Mitchell Shea

LCCN: 2020909707
ISBN: 978-1-7351181-0-9
ISBN-13: 978-1-7351181-1-6

Printed in the United States of America
First Edition 14 13 12 11 10 / 10 9 8 7 6 5 4 3 2 1

# DEDICATION

To my wife who puts up with all of my shenanigans.

# THE WAY OUT

# CONTENTS

# TO INFINITY AND BEYOND

## OCTOBER 2025

When her charming Southern lilt (that's how I imagine her voice) popped up on my screen, I shook off the daze that commonly drifts over me in these long stretches of darkness and silence. Though there is always something to monitor, always some measurement to take, some report to be filed, once you are moving away from the sun and it no longer rises and sets to mark the hours and the days, every task tends to bleed into the next. The only exception is when she makes her routine check-in at 0700 and I get a few minutes of contact with the world below.

No, I'm not alone up here. We have a crew of twenty-six—eighteen men and eight women. How do you like those odds? Yet another reason I look forward to hearing from my friend on the ground. And, when you're looking at being stuck on a spaceship with the same handful of people, day in and day out, on an expedition that's to last ten years, a fresh voice—even if there isn't a face to go with it, or actual sound—is most welcome.

Audrey Logan: *Martin? . . . Officer Lucas . . . how are we today? Running a little late?*

Martin Lucas: *Yeah, traffic's been extra heavy. But, except for a dustup with the Venusians over a petty right-of-way issue, it's all been pretty smooth. Just gridlocked. By the way, did you know they have extra middle fingers?*

Audrey Logan: *Make sure you document all of that in the log. We don't need an intergalactic incident. Those Venusians get overly passionate about everything.*

Martin Lucas: *So true!*

Audrey Logan: *Seriously, though, I need your report. We've been detecting some unusual energy pulses and the team wants to make some projections in case a course correction is needed.*

Our "witty" banter is the highlight of my day, so it's disappointing to have it cut short for business. But she's not wrong. Something wonky has been showing up in our readings and I've been watching and reporting to the captain. She says it could be anything—most likely disruptions from the asteroid field we passed a few days ago (well, to you guys on Earth it would have been a few months) that could be creating a ripple effect, kind of like what happens when a motorboat sends shock waves through the water as it speeds through. Even with all of the exploration we've done and the continual evaluation and calculation of what's going on up here, it's all still quite the mystery, since most of what we know is from the perspective of being essentially stationary on Earth. We really have no clue what we are going to encounter and experience as we careen through space. But, for me anyway, that's kind of the fun of it.

Still, this . . . anomaly? blip? hiccup? . . . I'm not really sure what to call it. I have to admit, it has me a little unnerved.

Martin Lucas: *Course correction?! There's a lot of course out here and not a lot of places to ask for directions if we take a wrong turn.*

Audrey Logan: *We won't let you wander too far away. How soon can you have those readings to me?*

Martin Lucas: *I'll run another report now and check in with Captain Halverson for her evaluation before sending. Give me an hour. Okay?*

Audrey Logan: *Alright, but that's an hour my time, not yours, right?*

Martin Lucas: *Time dilation doesn't really work that way. It's not noticeable in such small increments, but I should be able to have it to you by 0800 your time.*

Audrey Logan: *I'll be waiting.*

It is hard to maintain perspective when you are dealing with the oddities of space travel and what happens at near the speed of light. As I said, this mission is supposed to last ten years, but that's how it's going to feel on Earth. That's 4.24 light-years to travel to Alpha Centauri—oh, yeah, I guess I skipped that part; that's where we're headed. It's our closest neighbor and there is a little planet we call Proxima b that we think could possibly, maybe, perhaps support human life, so we're out here trying to see what's what, since we're making such a mess of things on the planet we already inhabit. But I digress. The world's astronomers have collected about as much useful data as they can through telescopes and estimations, so it's our mission to gather actual environmental samples, document climate observations, and other hands-on information. Once we get there, we'll spend approximately six months doing our research and begin the work of determining if it is inhabitable, and then 4.24 light-years back. The thing is, when you travel at the kinds of speeds that are necessary for any interstellar travel, this thing called time dilation happens. So, what feels like a little over four years to those on the ground is going to feel like about two years to us. I can't even begin to explain what that experience is like. I won't even really get it myself until we are back on Earth and get the full effect. But I better get to those reports or it's going to feel like I made her wait a week.

"Captain Halverson, you really need to see this."

"What is it, Lucas?"

"I was rerunning the reports to send to Ground Control and there has been a significant uptick in the energy pulse activity we've been tracking . . . like, a 30 percent change in the last four hours."

"Get Li, Awan, and Commander Young on deck now."

"Yes, ma'am."

I race down to the engineering deck to bring Michael Li, our crew physicist, and Kamil Awan, our head engineer, back to the bridge. I will admit that it didn't occur to me before jumping up out of my seat and rushing through the passage to the next module that I could have summoned them over the comms, but halfway there, it feels like the right decision anyway because I'm so amped up I would probably scare the crap out of everyone on the ship.

When I reach the engineering pod, the look on Michael's face tells me they've been watching this activity too and it isn't good.

"Captain wants you both on the bridge."

"We were just about to head that way. Kamil is making a few final calculations."

Kamil doesn't even look up at me, just holds up a single finger, urging me to give him another minute. We wait in silence and it feels like we just hit pause on the speed of light. I know I'm not doing an even remotely respectable job of hiding my impatience, but the fidgeting has a mind of its own.

Michael doesn't seem to be managing his anxiety any better than I am and we exchange silent glances that are loaded with frustration while Kamil does his thing. Finally, after what feels like eons, he slams down the pencil he's been using to scrawl a lot of numbers and shapes that are foreign to me, snatches up his papers, and blows past me to the door. I'd like to interject here that with the trillions of dollars we've spent on all of the technological advancements and unimaginable "futuristic" accomplishments that have brought us to this moment, I am deeply amused, and fairly sentimental, about the fact that he still uses the old-fashioned method of pencil and paper. (At least it's not an abacus!)

As I am musing about his antiquated computing techniques, Kamil turns back with annoyance and grunts, wondering why Michael and I are not on his heels. He's not one for in-depth verbal communication. I've been told countless times that I'm more of a talker than your average guy, but, really, I think he's said a total of fifty words to me in the two years I've known him.

Michael and I move toward him and we quickly make our way back to the bridge. I tell them to go on ahead so I can retrieve Commander Young from his quarters. He had been on the last shift and is not going to be happy I'm waking him. He's a great guy—the kind you definitely want in your corner in a crisis. From what I've heard, he flew some pretty gnarly missions with Captain Halverson in the Air Force before they joined NASA, so they are really tight. And that means they have a shorthand for communicating that can leave the rest of us in the dust. But he also strikes me as the type to shoot the messenger, so I'm going in on eggshells.

"So, what you're telling me is that these energy pulses aren't so much emitting outward toward us as they are going toward something else in the direction we are headed?"

Kamil speaks in a clipped Pakistani accent that diminishes in discernibility with his increasing fervor. "Yes, Captain, I hesitate to say it, but there is something on the horizon that seems to be drawing energy into it, not unlike a black hole."

"A black *fucking* hole?!" I shriek, hoping I just didn't hear him correctly through his accent, and then I quickly retreat to my station, trying to hide from the admonishing glare of everyone on deck.

"Awan, that is a term we don't throw around lightly out here," she says, acknowledging what everyone is thinking and what I blurted out; but she does it in a much more judicious way, as she would, being our leader for a reason. "Help me get clear on what we are dealing with here."

"My apologies, Captain, but based on the data we have, there is every possibility we have stumbled upon a recently collapsed star. It does not appear to be of a significant size; however, should it, in fact, be a black hole, the results are nonetheless catastrophic."

Right now I'm really wishing he would go back to being a man of few words.

"Li, do you concur with his findings?"

"Yes, Captain, I'm afraid, I do." Michael Li is a confident and articulate scientist who doesn't come off as a scientist at all. I know how that sounds; but, let's be honest, scientists have a very specific stereotype and the trend over the last decade of celebrity nerds, notwithstanding, this typecasting persists for a reason. The only exception is that he is very quick to correct you if you make the mistake of calling him Mike.

"Okay. Get this data transmitted to NASA now. It's going to take half an hour for them to receive the transmission, as it is. We need to get them working on a solution, or we won't have time for any course correction before it's too late."

There it is again, that term—*course correction*. Does no one else see how absurd it sounds? As if we could just take the next off-ramp and turn around or pull up our intergalactic Waze™ for an alternate route.

As Kamil joins me to begin relay of the data, Captain Halverson barks orders to the others on the team. I hear Commander Young swearing under his breath, wishing he could have stayed in bed, and again, I feel the need to duck in case he really is the shoot-the-messenger type.

I type as fast as I can to keep up with Kamil's dictation, and within five minutes, we hit "Send" on the transmission. And we wait.

You'd think we'd be springing to action to avoid the impending collision course with doom; but, as skilled as we are, we can't make a move without the input of the collective brain trust on the ground. We have one perspective; they have another. And both are needed in order to avoid setting us on a course for another potential disaster in the attempt to avert this one. All we can really do at this point is check and recheck readings, which is why Kamil and Michael slip away in silence to return to the engineering hub.

Being first pilot, I have to remain on the bridge and within the palpable tension between the captain and first commander as they weigh the options and the responsibility of numerous lives sitting squarely on their shoulders. I'd rather be where I could feel like I am being useful, but I guess being on hand to receive instructions from NASA is equally important. I have a feeling we are going to have mere seconds to act, once we have a plan.

"Captain, what are the odds we'll get out of this alive?"

"Lucas, that's not helpful."

"Sonja, look, the kid's got a point. We have to start thinking about how we want to go out if this goes sideways."

"Hunter, I don't need you going to the dark place right now. We do still have options right now. We don't even know for sure that what's out there is pulling us to our doom."

"What else could it be? I think everyone deserves to know what's coming so they can prepare—record goodbyes to family, get right with their god, whatever."

Well, that went well. I didn't expect my existential musings to trigger the commander that way. He's kind of a Negative Nancy, but I didn't expect him to be quite so fatalistic.

"Captain . . . Commander . . . risk . . . is our . . . business," I say in my best Captain Kirk impression, trying to lighten the mood. It doesn't land well. I guess I'll just be focusing on this monitor and see if I can will it to give us a message from the ground.

I've come to that place where everyone is wishing for a "Refresh" button to hit. We have been told to stand by and await instruction, but we have been bolting through space at 85 percent of the speed of light, racing toward an absolutely terrifying prospect. And, as instinctual as it might be to hit the brakes, at this trajectory, that doesn't happen without unimaginable repercussions. We have begun reducing our speed to buy some time, but the current conventional wisdom is that, if we are heading toward a black hole, we will need full thrust to avoid its gravitational pull, so slowing too much will prevent us from making that quick sidestep when it becomes necessary.

You're probably wondering why we haven't just turned around and gone home by now, or at least headed left or right, out of the path we are on. Well, first, have you ever tried to turn a ship on a dime? Doesn't happen. This vehicle is big, heavy, and doesn't have performance suspension. And at the rate of speed we have currently . . . well, I'd probably end up putting us in an epic spin cycle. Aside from that, we don't really know how big this thing is and if we are heading toward the center or just the edge. Taking a guess right now could send us right toward the middle of it when we were possibly in a position to skirt by it on one side or another. Then there's the other stuff that's out there. We need a full-scope assessment of what else we might encounter if we divert in one direction or another. Unfortunately, it's not like what you see in Sci-Fi movies and TV. We have significant limitations up here.

So we wait. But it isn't getting easier. That time dilation I mentioned? I think they don't factor in the impact of human emotion relative to the passage of time. In other words, when you're scared shitless and you're waiting for a lifeline, seconds tick by like hours. I've exhausted all of my distraction methods, and everyone else on the bridge is pacing now, making me even more twitchy. Captain Halverson is on her fourteenth lap when Kamil and Michael burst through the doors, nearly plowing into her as they shout and frantically wave papers. They are barely breathing, and flushed, which doesn't bode well.

"Captain! We cannot wait for a response from the ground. This activity is increasing exponentially," Kamil belches out in a frenzy.

"What are you talking about?"

"He's right, Captain," I shout as I realize our navigational controls are disabled. "I can't steer the ship, and our propulsion is accelerating. I'm trying to decelerate and it's not working!"

Captain Halverson is at my side in approximately a nanosecond and leans over me to read the display panel for herself. She begins shouting with remarkable composure into her comm.

"All personnel, we are experiencing system failure. Please secure in place and brace for impact." She repeats it, this time with dismay and resolution mixed in her voice, "All personnel, we are experiencing system failure. Please . . . secure in place . . . and brace for impact."

Another little insight about me: I'm an overgrown child and my sense of humor can put people off. So, even though I recognize how wholly inappropriate it is, I can't help but chuckle a little as her last words sound a lot like Kirk, albeit unintentionally.

She glares at me—probably very aware of where my mind went—and instructs me to connect her with Ground Control.

"But, Captain, they won't be able to hear us. They won't get the trans . . ."

"I know that, Martin. But I want to send a final communication."

"Yes, ma'am."

I wasn't sure what was coming next, but I knew it had to be bad, since she used my first name.

"Mission Control, this is Captain Sonja Halverson of the *Alpha Centauri I*. We are no longer able to await instruction on corrective measures. Our situation has devolved precipitously and we cannot control our navigational system. We are being drawn into the gravitational field of an unidentified celestial body. We do not expect to survive." Her voice is breaking, and I look up at her in awe as I see the cracks in her stoic veneer emerging. "Our mission has failed, but what we have learned will be invaluable for those brave enough to follow behind us. Transmission complete."

Captain Halverson moves to her seat and straps in, scanning the bridge to make sure that everyone is in place and secured. She nods to Commander Young, who simply returns the gesture, takes a deep breath, and exhales slowly.

Suddenly she turns to me and almost whispers, as if she is unsure of what she is about to say.

"Lucas, I want to try something."

"Yes, ma'am."

"Rev up the engines and go full throttle."

Commander Young and I both jerk our heads toward her in disbelief.

"But that will guarantee we are split apart at the seams."

"Not necessarily."

"Sonja . . . Captain . . . that's . . . So your plan is just to hasten the inevitable?"

"Maybe not, Hunter. I'm no astrophysicist, but I do know about the theories around spinning black holes . . . maybe, just maybe, if we get lucky and this is that kind of black hole, we'll come out with only a few bumps and bruises. We . . . I . . . have to try something."

"Well, we're not getting out of this alive regardless. Might as well give it a shot. Go down fighting. Lucas, make it so."

As scary as all of this is, I still can't restrain the massive eye roll that comes over me with that one. It's okay for him, but not okay for me? I guess he gets to be whatever kind of tool he wants to be in the last moments of his life. Who's gonna be around to call him on it?

So I suck in as much resolve as I can and throw the switch. And here's the thing, when you are already at a velocity of 570 million miles per hour, and then you add thrusters to it, it's not like hitting the gas in your car. The jolt forward is exponentially more powerful. Not as bad as hitting the brakes, but it's jarring. And when I say the *whoosh* is something I will never forget, it's only meaningless because of the minuscule amount of time I have left to remember it.

In fact, as this thought forms in my head, everything is going dark and I . . .

*Dear Reader,*

*What follows is a collection of interviews with individuals, attempting to piece together what happened to the* Alpha Centauri I *crew on that fateful day in the beginning phase of their mission.*

*Initially this was a personal project, a pursuit to satisfy my own curiosity. However, it quickly turned into a quest, a mission to expose wrongs multiple governments tried to bury. The interviews were collected over several weeks, and the people who have spoken with us did so with the understanding that what they shared would not be made public for two years after our conversations. You will come to understand why this was necessary and why this specific amount of time was designated.*

*While many questions remain unanswered, one thing is clear: The world and the future we have before us were changed by this group of men and women in ways we may never be able to fully account for. Some of this will surely sound like the stuff of Science Fiction . . . and, certainly, it is. However, we have only glimpsed the horizon of what lies out there by accidentally stumbling onto what already is. What we learn from this remains to be seen, but it is not simply the folly of an overactive imagination. That much we know.*

*My goal as a documentarian has been to gather as many perspectives as possible to fill in gaps where one person's perspective ends and another begins, and to confirm as many details as possible. My purpose has been to give us all some insight into their lives and how they were impacted in order to examine a broader theme: the hidden costs associated with pursuing our ambitions. You've probably heard the old adage "Be careful what you wish for; you just might get it." Well, I don't know of a more perfect illustration of this truth than the story you are about to read.*

*A lot of things seem like a good idea in theory. Sometimes it pans out. Sometimes finding out just isn't worth it. You can be the judge.*

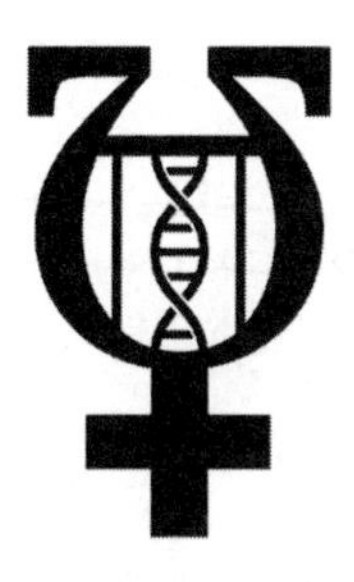

# CHAPTER ONE
## A NOT SO WARM WELCOME

Amelia Corcoran (AC): Yeah, so I was just starting my shift and trying to tidy up the place so I could review the overnight reports and begin running new calculations. You know, once, just once, it would have been nice to come in and not find the place trashed by the night shift. Those guys acted like they still lived in their mother's basements and . . . okay, well, they do. But, still, they really needed to start learning how to clean up after themselves. I get that staying awake all night can be hard, and involves lots of caffeine and sugar, but my fingers should not stick to the dang keyboard in someone else's mess!

I was wishing I'd have time to write up a complaint or something, but I had all these other reports to do because they didn't finish their job . . . again. I mean, how hard is it to watch a screen and make a note of any crap that falls out of the sky? This job was boring and tedious, but it wasn't hard. Sometimes I really wished something interesting would drop in on us . . .

*I'm sorry, could we back up a minute and start with an introduction? I'd like to get your name, age, and occupation on record.*

AC: Oh. Yeah. My name is Amelia Corcoran. I'm twenty-four years old, and I worked as a Deep Space Scanning Specialist at the Space Flight Operations Facility in Pasadena, California.

*Great. Thank you. So you were saying you'd come in for your shift and were cleaning up after your coworkers?*

AC: Yeah. And I complained about it to my supervisor, Ms. Harden. She got kind of snippy with me because all she wanted to know about was what I had observed and why she'd had to come in to the office on a Saturday. Sheesh! You know, nothing interesting ever happened around there, so you'd think they'd cut a girl a little slack. I'm a storyteller; context matters to me. But she didn't look like she was interested in any of that, so I cut to the chase. I told her I was scanning the western quadrant of the 22$^{nd}$ parallel.

*Where is that?*

AC: The Pacific Ocean . . . near Hawaii. Anyway, I saw lots of asteroids and junk falling into our atmosphere. It was pretty much my whole job. It happened (still happens) every day. But . . . not like this. We mostly focus on 750 to 800 kilometers when scanning for orbital debris . . . that's around 500 miles up . . .

*Oh, why do you stop there?*

AC: Well, we don't sweep beyond the exosphere with as much frequency, since we don't really have to be concerned about any debris until it gets below that. But we do check for outlying debris of a significant size to determine what we might need to monitor as it approaches the atmosphere. Side note: When I started explaining this to Ms. Harden, she said, "Amelia, I am your boss. I did not get here by not knowing anything about science or what you do. We are working on a clock here, so I need you to cut to the chase." She could be so . . . supervisor-ish sometimes.

Anyway, I was doing one of those scans days earlier and I detected a very large object moving through the asteroid belt and it did not look like any hunk of rock I'd ever seen out there. I paused for dramatic effect, but Ms. Harden let me know pretty quickly it wasn't very effective. So I continued. Honestly, if I didn't know better, I'd say it just showed up out of nowhere. Still, the velocity didn't seem concerning.

*Why is that?*

AC: Well, the manned spacecraft were traveling way faster than this before . . . um, you know . . .

*Oh, yeah. I get it.*

AC: I checked again that morning and it was within the lunar orbit, and that's when I really got interested. I sent out a beacon just for grins and giggles. And, would you believe, the radio started crackling then? I heard, "Ground, do you read?" over and over. I wasn't sure what to do at first. I mean, I didn't know of anything, or any*one*, that was supposed to be out there. I said, "Hello," and he started freaking out and I didn't know what else to say, so that's when I called Ms. Harden.

*How did she respond? Did it seem like it alarmed her?*

AC: Well, she was still asleep when I called her and it only took her about thirty minutes to get dressed and drive to Pasadena from West LA. Even with lighter weekend traffic, that's still lightning speed. I gave her the rundown when she got there. They kept transmitting every few minutes, but I didn't know what I was supposed to say to them. And the guy . . . the one calling to Ground Control . . . he kept calling me Audrey . . . he kept saying, "Audrey, is that you?" Who the heck is Audrey?

*Who is Audrey?*

AC: Damned if I know. Ms. Harden didn't know either, but she said I did the right thing in alerting her. She said they had a team on the way, and I could just stand down for the time being. She would take it from there. I asked if I could stick around to see what happened. I mean, was I really supposed to just go home with such a big mystery unsolved? And, believe me, it was *B-I-G*, big. If there was any doubt about that, what happened next made it clear. She told me I actually needed to stick around in case they needed to ask me more questions. And then she told me to just stay out of the way.

*So, what did happen next?*

AC: She nudged me away from my station, and started trying to communicate with whoever it was while I just sat there, indulging my OCD, cleaning between the keys of the keyboard on another station, and we waited for the higher-ups to descend on the place.

*Was she able to communicate with them?*

AC: Yeah. She started saying, "Ground Control to . . . um, spacecraft, please identify yourself." She turned to me and shrugged her shoulders, like she didn't have any more of a clue about what to say to them than I did. I mean, I could have done that. Heck, I *was* doing that before she got there.

*What happened when the bosses' bosses got there?*

AC: They all came in and took over the place, set up camp in the conference room, and then they called me in and started grilling me. One guy, in particular, kept repeating the same question . . . "Are you *sure* he said *'Alpha Centauri I,'*" as if I might change the answer after the fifth time. And I mean, I knew it was a big, big deal . . . but I really couldn't believe it was for real. It had to be a hoax or an elaborate prank. But all the suits had their underwear in a twist over it, so something made them think it was real.

They were on a conference call with some muckety-mucks in DC for at least half an hour without telling me or Ms. Harden anything. I don't like not being in the know, so when they finally came back out to ask me once again to tell them what I saw and heard, I asked, "What's going on? Why are you guys acting like . . . well, like someone rose from the dead?"

*Were you able to get an answer from them?*

AC: Yeah, Ms. Harden—after kind of looking at me like my hair was on fire—said, "Well, Amelia . . . that's because that's exactly what we are seeing."

*That must have been a shock.*

AC: Boy, was it. She went into a bit of a history lesson I didn't actually need, but I let her go on explaining how the *Alpha Centauri I* was a manned expedition sent out in 2025 with the mission of exploring Proxima b to determine if the environment was compatible with human life.

*It was a huge leap forward in space exploration from what I understand. I'm a good bit older than you are, but I am still too young to remember much about it. In fact, it happened just a few months before I was born.*

AC: Yeah, I wasn't close to being born yet, but it was covered in my history classes in school, and then, of course, I learned more about it when I trained to take this job. But I just couldn't imagine this was *that* ship. It was sucked into a black hole and disappeared. I was convinced someone with too much time on their hands was messing with us. Apparently, they didn't agree and felt from what they were able to assess this was credible. Guess that's why they make the big bucks.

*It was an alarming development. Everyone thought they evaporated into space forty years ago. It was inconceivable.*

AC: That's when I started to get why those suited-up old people were having such a hard time. It was way before my time and *I* couldn't comprehend it. Heck, they probably knew someone on that ship! I asked Ms. Harden what they wanted me to do next because that guy was still asking for Audrey. At first, I thought maybe we were getting some wires crossed with some other radio frequency, but I began to wonder if he . . . Martin . . . thought I was someone he talked to before.

*You seemed to be holding back a smile just then. What was that about?*

AC: Oh, that. Yeah, I'm a nervous laugher. Also, my brain tends to think inappropriate things under stress, so every time I heard him say his name, I kept thinking, *Martin the Martian is trying to talk to me from outer space.* Also, he sounds cute . . . and available—something that has been in really short supply down here lately.

*Who?*

AC: Actually, it was Marvin, not Martin. It's from a cartoon my grandma showed me when I was little and really into space stuff. I guess it's no surprise I ended up working here. Anyway, Ms. Harden told me I needed a little decorum in front of the brass, and she also needed me to keep my composure as we figured out next steps. Like I'm actually part of that "we." She also told me in no uncertain terms that I was not to talk to anyone about this. She said we would be on lockdown until they could assess the situation and the full ramifications. In fact, she told me to prepare to be there at the facility a few days while they did what they had to do to contain the situation. They couldn't risk word of this getting out.

*How long did they keep you there?*

AC: Long enough that it was a good thing I decided not to get a dog.

*Hmm. That wasn't a very direct response. Is there something you'd like to say about that?*

AC: I'm really not supposed to. Let's move on.

*[She looked very much like she wanted to tell me more, but she had been through a lot by the time I interviewed her and I got the sense I needed to tread carefully.]*

*Okay. Fair enough. Tell me what you can about what happened next.*

AC: Over the next eight hours a steady stream of people who seemed to think they were impressive arrived here and overtook our station. They commandeered all of our workspace, barked orders, and locked themselves in the conference room, only sticking a head out to bark more orders. I made lots of coffee and ordered takeout and waited in the wings, watching as they (grown men and women) made even more of a mess in a couple of hours with their food wrappers and coffee mug rings on the table than the night crew did in a month. I knew I was going to be the one to clean up their profoundly inconsiderate eating habits. Everything was in a frenzy and they actually put a countdown clock up on the big screen in the control room."

*So you normally didn't see this level of activity in your office?*

AC: No way. Our facility is where the Jet Propulsion Laboratory and NASA's Deep Space Network are housed, but there just wasn't much happening here after the *Alpha Centauri I* disappeared. Oh, hey, want to know an interesting little factoid? As it turns out, this was also where Audrey worked back in the day. I wondered if they would bring her in or other people who worked here then, but they didn't.

*Whoa. That's quite a coincidence*!

AC: I mean, I guess not really. It makes sense that she would have been in this location because she did a lot of the same job I have been doing. She just had some interesting stuff to monitor and someone real to communicate with.

*Good point. So you mentioned putting a clock up on the screen. What was that for?*

AC: To keep track of their guesstimate of when they would "touch down." They figured it would be somewhere in the Pacific, off the coast of California, so ours was definitely as good a command center as they could hope for under the circumstances. When they put up the clock, they were estimating arrival in T-minus not much longer. The ship had been moving along through space at a pretty good clip, but, based on the reports they were giving us, they were operating on severely diminished engine power, so their momentum was mostly coming from whatever trajectory they had from being belched out of who knows where.

*That must have been terrifying for everyone.*

AC: This much I know: The laws of physics tell you that a body in motion stays in motion until something intervenes to stop it. The trouble was, they weren't going to encounter that until they hit our atmosphere and experienced gravity and drag. Gravity was going to want to pull them right to the surface (which we were hoping would be the ocean), but the friction that happens as something hits our wind currents creates drag, which, god willing, would slow them down. Killing the engines was only going to do so much, since they weren't providing enough power to do more than steer as it was. I could go into a bunch of other physics stuff, but it's not going to get you any closer to understanding what was happening.

*That's fine. I'm sure the readers and viewers will appreciate the simplicity.*

AC: By the way, who is going to see this?

*No telling really. At this point I'm just documenting this for historical purposes. It may just sit in a library somewhere, but who knows. So, back to the countdown . . .*

AC: Yeah, so the big debate moved from whether it was legit to how to get them on the ground as safely as possible, and then to what happened next—how would we retrieve them and the ship without a lot of people noticing, where would we put them (if they survived), and what would we do with them after that. I know. Just a few little logistical kinks, right? I guessed they would at least go to Miramar first. It was one of only three military bases still operational out here in the West, and there was a medical facility there, so they could get assessments and any necessary treatment. I asked Ms. Harden if I was right in that assumption, and she said we were not on the Need-to-Know list. Like I didn't know I was just a peon, but *I* found them. Shouldn't I have gotten to know what happened to them?

*Sounds fair to me. They were pretty secretive about all of it, weren't they? Did that bother you, or were you used to that being in government work?*

AC: Are you kidding me? I went to work every day expecting to be fired because I was being insubordinate. I never got used to it. But this was way beyond just grumbling or staging a protest to get heard. This was code-word clearance kind of stuff. At one point I was summoned by one of the suits who just stuck her head out of the cave. I have to say, it astounds me that after all these years of the women running the show, we can still be treated in such a condescending way . . . and by our own team!

*I guess rudeness isn't gender specific.*

AC: Definitely not. So she looked at me pretty smugly like she was expecting a *ma'am* when I spoke to her, but I didn't give her the satisfaction. After a few seconds she finally asked me if I was the one who detected the ship. Then she asked me to put together a report of when it was first detected, at least an estimated rate of speed, and distance traveled to the moment. Man, did it nearly send me through the roof when she kind of looked down her nose at me and said, "Do you think you can do that?" Of course I can. It's my *job*. Ugh. So she said they needed it in fifteen minutes and then retreated to the room of the privileged and closed the door once again, without waiting for my answer. The good thing was, I'd already done that work, since, as I said, it's my job. I just did a quick update to determine where they were currently and hit "Print." I scanned the report as I walked to the conference room, and—oh, boy—did it send shock waves through me.

*Why? What did the report tell you?*

AC: While their rate was declining somewhat, it wasn't at a ratio that was very comforting. Like they say, "It's not the fall that kills you; it's the sudden stop." And this one was looking to be a doozy. When I got a couple feet away from the door, it was clear the same woman who asked for the update was waiting impatiently at the door because she flung it open before I could knock and held out her hand. When I handed it over, she made eye contact with me for the first time. She read everything she needed to know on my face without even looking at the report. I saw the first traces of humanity register at that moment, and we both knew this was shaping up to be a tragedy. And . . . then she slammed the door in my face. I get there was all kind of intensity around this; but is courtesy and common decency impossible? I really thought the kinder, gentler way of being was kind of the norm these days in this New World Order. But, I guess, people in power, regardless of gender, can be infected by the ugly side of it.

*So, how far away were they at that point?*

AC: I think they spent another fifteen minutes sequestered and then everyone gathered in the control room to watch the clock tick away the remaining minutes until arrival. It felt like everyone was afraid to breathe, as though a sharp exhale could somehow throw them off course. The tension soared really high the moment the ship reached the S-band communication blackout.

*And that is?*

AC: Basically, when a spacecraft returns to our atmosphere, they are going so fast that a ton of heat and pressure are generated. That causes a reaction that disrupts electronic communications for around three minutes. I'd never been around for something like that, but it apparently freaks everyone out enough that they've been trying to find a solution for as long as we've been going to space. And that's where we were. Radio silence. We expected to reestablish communication within a few seconds, but it wasn't going to mean a lot as far as helping them get to ground safely. We just got to talk to them until one thing or another happened. It really was a miracle they survived as long as they did and made it back here. We all were thinking, but no one was saying, how much it would suck if they came all this way not to make it all the way home.

*Yes, that would have been a really tragic irony.*

AC: And here's the other thing that kinda sucked. They were keeping me around to keep word from getting out, but also so I could talk to the first pilot. That was Martin. He thought I was the tech he used to work with. They—the suits—wanted me to let him continue with this delusion so no one on the ship really knew what was going on down here. I hated it, but the order came down from the top—Madam President—that they weren't supposed to get any information until we could get them into a secured facility. I guess I see the logic. They had enough to panic over just getting back down to Earth. But I don't like lying to people. I come from a long line of activists who all groomed the next generations to "speak truth to power" from the moment they could talk. My mom did it with me and she has never liked the fact that I work for "the man," even if that man is a woman now. But my mouth still gets me in trouble, which is a source of pride for her. I guess she consoles herself by telling herself and her friends that I'm changing the system from within. I don't know about all of that, but I am developing a reputation for being "challenging." I'd probably be out of a job if there were any competition.

*So, how did you handle communicating with Martin?*

AC: Well, his now-familiar voice was crackling through static and it was hard to understand him. I assumed he would be having the same difficulty hearing me, so I let that be my cover. They told me not to use his name or anything, just find out their status. So I just tried to keep the focus on them.

*I have a transcript of the call.*

AC: You do? I don't even remember what I said.

*It went like this:*

*Ground:* Alpha Centauri I, *do you read?*
*Alpha: Yes . . . hello . . . yes . . . Audrey?*
*Ground:* Alpha Centauri I, *how are you?*
*Alpha: Everything is still intact, so I guess we are good.*
*Ground: Based on current speed and trajectory, we project your landing site to be in the Pacific Ocean, off the coast of California. We have naval ships in the vicinity and the Coast Guard ready to move in and intercept once you touch down.*
*Alpha: Well, let's just hope there's something left to retrieve.*

AC: The room fell silent because everyone recognized there was a good chance there wouldn't be, but nobody wanted to say it. After what seemed like several minutes of dead quiet, but probably was only about three seconds, Martin chimed in again and said, "Sorry. I know that was dark, but you should know by now that's how I roll. I have to say, if we make it out of this, the thing I'm looking forward to most is putting a face with the disembodied voice I talked to for so many months." I just sort of laughed because I couldn't bring myself to say more.

*That must have been unnerving.*

AC: I think I should back up a bit and explain for anyone who hears or reads this later and doesn't know what we were up against that we were kind of flying blind for more reasons than being caught off guard by the reappearance of this ship.

*Okay, good. That will be helpful.*

AC: Due to a series of unfortunate events that I won't go into because they cover several decades, most of the space exploration program was put on hold some time ago. A big part of it was because the *Alpha Centauri I* and its crew of twenty-six disappeared, and the tragedy created a pretty big scandal. It was a major point of contention at the time, lots of protests, lobbying of Congress, etc. But, in the end, everyone in charge felt it wasn't worth the risk to continue efforts to explore space further, considering all the other things we had to contend with at the time. So, the most we've done in the space program lately is study what we've learned from previous expeditions, map the galaxy further, and what I've been doing—monitor the skies for any debris or other celestial stuff that could present an issue.

*What would that be? Are you saying there are aliens out there?*

AC: Oh, I wouldn't begin to make a guess about that. I'm talking old satellites, the parts that break away from rockets launched into space, meteors—just cosmic trash that floats around out there until it gets close enough to the earth's gravitational pull, and then heads in our direction. You don't hear about a lot of flaming things falling from the sky. A conspiracy nutjob would tell you it's because we're keeping the UFO landings a secret. The reality is most of this junk burns up as it passes through the atmosphere and doesn't actually make it to the ground. But I do like to have fun with people at parties. Okay . . . that's a lie. I don't go to parties.

*So that's a* no *on the aliens?*

AC: Like I said, I'm not going on record with a guess about that. Anyway, since we've not put anyone in space since this crew, things haven't changed a ton. There really hasn't been any need to develop any new methods or technology—not that there is funding for it anyhow. So, based on old data, in most cases, the whole landing process after hitting our atmosphere is supposed to take about thirteen and a half minutes total. Since their craft is all but disabled, we didn't really know how all that was going to go, which is why we were basically just crossing our fingers and hoping for the best. We thought they might have drag chutes they could deploy.

*Didn't you have the schematics of the ship to know for sure?*

AC: Oh, yeah. They were equipped with them; we just didn't know how much of the craft was actually functional and our ability to communicate with them was so limited, we never got around to asking. So I talked them down once the comms came back online. I think I said something like, "Yeah, we will be glad to have you safely on land. Um . . . hang in there. It shouldn't be much longer." I know. Lame, right? His response was just as lame though . . . "Thanks, see you in a few." But, I mean, really, what do you say?"

*I'm not sure what I would say. I know it's time for you to get going, so let's bring this in for a landing . . . pardon the pun.*

AC: Wow. Okay. Since we didn't have any visual contact, all the big screen displayed was an altitude graph with an icon moving gradually closer and closer to the surface. We all watched the little blip intently and silently. I heard Martin say, "Audrey, I think I see . . ." and then the communication went out. Eyes darted around the room searching for a clue about what happened. But not a word or sound was uttered. We were just frozen. I noticed a few avoiding the furtive glances from the rest of us, and I hoped it didn't mean what I thought it meant. That activism gene I mentioned . . . had my Spidey senses tingling, and I didn't like it, but there was nothing I could do at that point but wait to see how it would shake out. There was no telling how long it would take for us to get a report from the rescue team, so we just sat in silence. Did I mention I'm not good at waiting?

*Hold on, what triggered your . . . um . . .* Spidey *senses?*

AC: Sorry. That's going to have to be for another conversation.

# CHAPTER TWO
## ROCKY REENTRY

*Commander Hunter Young, thank you for speaking with me. May I call you Hunter?*

Hunter Young (HY): Might as well. I don't stand much on formality anymore.

*Great. So, could you tell me, Hunter, what happened after the ship landed?*

HY: Yeah, it was a bitch of an impact and it took a bit before any of us started coming around—I didn't have any way to tell how long we were out. I think I may have been the first. I started calling out for Sonja—Captain Halverson—and Martin, our first pilot. There were two others on the bridge with us, Charles Du Plessis, the security chief, and Erica Steele, one of the other officers. I couldn't even tell if anyone besides me was still breathing and I was afraid to move. I remember just talking myself through it. I told myself to start at the toes and wiggle. They worked, so I moved to the fingers. Check. Lift the arms . . . slowly. Whoa. My ol' body had only experienced simulated gravity for a long time, and there are differences for sure. The things you take for granted.

*So you were uninjured? That's good.*

HY: Yeah, got tossed about a little, but no worse for wear. Once I did a head-to-toe assessment and knew I was good, I told myself, *Young, get yourself out of this harness and check on your crew.* That's when I heard someone groan, but I couldn't tell who. As I looked around, I could see puddling from water seeping in from somewhere and so I just got moving. I felt around for the latch to my harness. It was a little jammed, but came loose with a good tug, and I was free. I ran over to Sonja and tried shaking her a little to get her to wake up. At first, there was no response and my heart nearly stopped, but pretty quickly her eyes fluttered open. Man, I don't think I have ever been so glad to see those icy blue eyes glaring back at me. We all got our bells rung in the splashdown, but I could tell she took a blow from somewhere else. She could too. She lifted her hand to the side of her head and I could see her fingers were coated in blood. It didn't seem to be life-threatening, but I had a feeling that if the rescue team didn't come soon, it could have been. I told her not to move. I was going to check on the rest of the team. She nodded her head and blanched almost immediately. It made me think my original assessment might be wrong and I started to stay, but she shooed me away with her hand. I knew then she'd be fine.

*What about the others on the bridge? And what about the ship itself? You said you were taking on water?*

HY: Yeah, things didn't come apart at the seams, like I expected, but there was an obvious crack in the hull and plenty of debris to trip over as I moved around to check on the others. Lucas was the next to stir. I checked in to make sure he was good and helped him get free of his harness. I told him I was moving on to the engineering bay and that he needed to keep an eye on Captain Halverson. He was a little slow on the uptake and it took a minute to register what happened, but he got to work quickly. I asked him to get me a sit rep on the rest of the cabin and an ETA on that rescue team, then headed to the door. I felt really foolish as I instinctively hit the panel to open it.

*What happened? Was it jammed?*

HY: No. Weren't you paying attention? We didn't have any juice. I had to pry it open manually—time I didn't need to lose.

*Wow. Okay. Sorry about that.*

HY: No, man, I'm sorry. I'm still a little on edge from the whole ordeal.

*Don't worry about it. So, how did you get the door open?*

HY: They have an emergency release built in, but my brain was so scrambled, I forgot about it. Then I couldn't find it. It was really frustrating. I'm trained for managing a crisis, but none of that seemed to be serving me in that moment. I finally figured it out, just not without panicking for a few minutes first, which was really embarrassing for me. Fortunately, no one was paying any attention. When I got the door opened and moved out into the corridor, everything was eerily quiet. I didn't like the . . . Well, I was going to say "the sound of it," but that's stupid.

*Not really. It's a common expression.*

HY: Anyway, thankfully, the engineering bay door was open when I got there, so I shouted in to Li and Awan to find out if their team was intact.

*Um, checking my notes . . . that's Michael Li and Kamil Awan?*

HY: Yeah, our resident nerds. Li is a physicist and Awan was our head engineer. They had five other people under them in engineering—a couple other engineers, another physicist, a botanist, and a chemist. Some of them were on the crew, not so much for the trip, but for what their expertise would offer when we got to Proxima. Do you need their names for the record?

*Oh, I think I have them . . . Uh, Byron Rice, Scott Jordan, Leila Tate, Javier Romero, and . . .*

HY: Latham.

*Yes, Kenneth Latham. He was a loaner from British Aeronautics, right?*

HY: Yeah, sharp guy. We had a few others on the crew from different countries. It was a really well-rounded group.

*It certainly seems so. What other nations were represented?*

HY: Well, we had a mixture of people of different races and backgrounds, but as far as those who weren't actually American citizens, we had a medical assistant—Yoshi Tanaka—from Japan and Daniel Cohen, in communications, from Israel. Charles Du Plessis, our security chief, was originally from South Africa, and Kamil was originally from Pakistan, but they had become US citizens a long time—decades—before the mission, so I guess they don't really count on this.

*Thanks for that. It sounds like a really diverse group of people.*

HY: It was. So, anyway, Li responded and said he was okay, just a little sore, but Kamil wasn't moving yet. I told him to see if he could suss out his condition and check on the rest of his team, and I'd swing back by for a report after I went down to medical to check on them. I have to tell you, when you're living in space with this many people, no ship is big enough to not feel like you're right on top of everyone, but in those moments when I was trying to assess the situation, everything felt miles apart. Closing the 20-yard distance between engineering and medical felt like it took an eternity.

*Was everyone okay when you got to medical?*

HY: Well, the door there was jammed, so it took even longer to find out. I shouted to Abe through the door to—yeah, I know, pointless. These things are airtight. But, as I pulled the release and began to shove, it seemed to move easier than on the bridge. As it inched open, I saw a pair of fingers reaching through to help me move the door out of the way. Abe and I looked at each other and just let out a collective sigh of relief.

*That's Dr. Abe Tilden, the medical director.*

HY: Yeah. I asked him what the situation was in there. He said, Sarah . . . that's his wife and head nurse . . . was fine and checking on the two patients they had in there. The lab technicians and assistants were all present and accounted for. He asked if I'd encountered anyone in need of medical attention. I told him about the captain's head injury, that she was bleeding but conscious and communicative when I left her with Lucas. I told him I was making the rounds and would try to assemble everyone in one location so we could deploy the rafts and get off the sinking ship. He started collecting a pretty stereotypical-looking medical bag as we talked, and then he asked Sarah to wait there while he went to the bridge and told her I would come back by and help her move everyone. He ran past me and it definitely made me feel better knowing he was on his way to check on Sonja. Lucas is a capable guy, but only at flying a ship, not dressing a head wound.

*How many other departments did you have to check on?*

HY: Two. I told Sarah I was heading down to the galley and then communications and would be bringing everyone back to the bridge. I asked her about the status of the patients and what kind of transport they might need. I knew they had two there. She said they would be fine to move. Their symptoms were chalked up to what we were calling reentry sickness. Headaches, vomiting, dehydration. She said they would be mobile. She is a sweet lady. Never figured her for being able to handle something like this though. Honestly, I didn't really think spouses should be on the team either, but she's stronger than she seems. They are a solid couple, that's for sure.

*Yes, I plan to talk with them later. They have an interesting story outside of this whole saga.*

HY: Definitely. So I went to the other areas and found everyone in good shape and started rounding them up. The bridge was barely big enough to hold all twenty-six members of the crew—standing room only, really—

but it was the best place to work from. Corralling everyone there went a lot faster than I expected. Within twenty minutes of splashdown, I had everyone in one place, which may not seem that impressive in a craft half the size of a football field, but in a situation like this, it would have been like herding cats.

*That was fast. Everyone cooperated?*

HY: Oh, yeah, we functioned like a well-oiled machine. That's why we were sent into space together. We trained for months together to be able to operate as a team. You don't go into something like this, with so many unknowns, without first getting everyone in sync as much as possible.

*Sure. Makes sense. Your training was, what? About eighteen months?*

HY: That's right. We had to learn how to operate the ship, put together plans for how to execute our mission once we got there. And we were going to be the only ones (at least that was the theory) on this isolated planet far from home. We had to make sure we could work well together for long stretches.

*And it was just you and the crew that whole time?*

HY: Well, we were allowed to come and go. It's not like we were in isolation the whole time. We had our individual homes and some semblance of a life outside of the training, but it was intensive for sure. So we had everyone collected and I asked Lucas what he'd been able to find out. He said they hadn't been able to reestablish communication with Ground. But, he pointed out, they had said they had rescue teams on standby in the area. He figured they were capable of traveling 28 to 30 knots at best and were probably about 100 miles out to give us wide berth. His best guess was that they were still three hours away.

*That seems like a long time to wait for a rescue. How fast is 30 knots anyway?*

HY: It definitely wasn't a number I enjoyed hearing, but let's be realistic. It's about 35 miles an hour. It's not like they could come in with those speedboats that go 300 miles per hour.

*Wow. I guess I never thought about how slow a big boat moves. So you had some time to kill. What did you do?*

HY: Well, Sonja, sporting a dramatic-looking bandage around her head thanks to Abe, was attempting to remain in control and began barking orders, saying, "We can't stay here. The water has already risen several inches. Commander Young, pull together a crew to deploy the life rafts and we'll move everyone there. Make sure we have medical represented on each one and distribute the injured and infirm across them." I had to remind her that included her. Of course she fought me on it. She said, "I will be here giving orders and will board last . . . as a good captain should. Now get moving." I could tell she had limited capacity, but I knew her all too well and decided it was best to let her do what she could. So I indulged her illusion of being in control and told Lucas to start dividing people into groups. I planned to do a roll call as we loaded everyone. I told Li to come with me and grab a couple of the engineers and someone from communications for the next tasks so we could hurry up and wait.

*You and the captain have worked together for a long time, right? How is it serving under a woman? Do you work well together?*

HY: Sure, we are pretty tight and are usually on the same page. I don't have an issue with female leadership. We only run into trouble when her stubborn streak makes her think she's invincible. I pulled her aside before I left and tried to talk some sense into her. I said, "Sonja, I get the whole 'captain going down with the ship' thing, but I don't know what we're looking at here, and these people are going to need some guidance and a lot of morale boosting. I'll handle the logistics, but you need to reassure them, and you can't do that if you stay behind to the end. Now, I know you're going to say that I'm out of line, but they need you. We've been to hell and back and made it home by your quick thinking and the grace of some god out there. Let's not let it all fall apart in the last mile."

*How did she take that?*

HY: Abe had moved in next to me and chimed in with his own opinion. He said, "Captain, I agree with the commander. You have a nasty head wound, and as admirable as it is to put on a brave face, you need more than I can give you under these circumstances. There are others in your crew with medical needs as well. We need you to lead by example and get yourself to safety, which means off this deck, off this ship, where there are many hazards, seen and unseen. I know you outrank me, but as a doctor I am giving you orders to not be a martyr here." Abe is kind of our elder statesman, on top of being a doctor, so that helped me make my case. Sonja made a big show of not liking it, but she gave in. She said since her head was pounding, if it would shut the two of us up, she would go when everyone else was ready. But she had to get in one last assertion of her authority by ordering me to go get us ready to disembark . . . which I would have been already doing if she hadn't tied me up with her nonsense.

*Hmm. I can see how frustrating it is when someone doesn't take orders.*

HY: Okay, I see what you're doing there. And, yeah, we butt heads sometimes. I'm not the best at just rolling over, which made my life in the military a lot harder than it was for others. However, enough about that. I took Li and the group he assembled down to the docking module to prep the rafts and open the hatch to inflate them. On the way down, one of the communications officers informed me that our connection with Ground Control was cut—"unexpectedly interrupted" is the way he put it—before we were out of the thermosphere. I didn't have the time to focus on that in the moment, and I told myself it could have been a glitch, trying to get my mind back on the task at hand. But my gut kept screaming at me that it wasn't. I was barely containing the panic, as it was, so I ordered him not to tell anyone else. Thankfully, the cargo bay was intact and we were able to release the hatch with no problem. We were bobbing on the surface of the water, but I knew it wouldn't last. We had four rafts that could hold ten people each, and I figured we would need some supplies since there was no telling how long it would actually take them to get to us.

*Good thinking. Sounds like you really were trained well.*

HY: Yep. That military training always seems to come in handy. I told Harris—that's Steven Harris, one of our communications officers . . .

*Was he the one who pointed out the glitch?*

HY: Huh? Oh, no, that was Pearce Johnson, the lead on that team. Harris is just an operator. So I told Harris to go up to the galley and get some desalination kits. I didn't want to weigh down the rafts with water when we were sitting on a literal ocean of it. And rations. I figured enough for everyone for two days to be safe.

*Two days?!*

HY: That was Harris's response too. As I told him, It was just an abundance of caution and not to freak out on me. Then I asked Scott Jordan, one of the engineers Li brought, to see if he could locate anything like a tarp we could use to shield us from the sun. I told Li to try to find a radio or something that might allow us to communicate with the outside world, and then go back to the bridge and tell Dr. Tilden to pull together some medical supplies. They all started to head in different directions, but I pulled them back to tell them, "Remember, keep what you heard to yourselves. We have to get everyone to safety, and then we'll figure out what the hell is going on." They all nodded and went on to take care of business.

*Would you like to take a break for a few minutes? I know you've been through quite an ordeal and must be exhausted.*

HY: Nah. I'm good. Where should we pick up? I guess I don't need to give you the whole play-by-play. I'll skip ahead to when we were moving everyone to the rafts.

*Sure, that sounds good. How long did that take?*

HY: I think it was about an hour after we landed . . . or *crashed* is probably more accurate. I started directing people. I wanted one person from medical on each raft. I assigned Sarah to go with Group One, Abe with Group Two, Nancy, Group Three, and then Yosh and Natalie with Group Four. I also wanted one member of the bridge crew on each, so I had Charles take the first raft. I put Captain Halverson on raft two, Lucas raft three, and I was on four. I delegated to Lucas to assign the rest of the crew to different rafts and turned my attention to making sure the supplies were evenly dispersed.

*An impressive coordination of efforts there. So you had an hour down, and I guess about two hours to go at that point?*

HY: That's definitely what we were expecting. We sheltered under a wing while the craft was still afloat to protect us from the blazing sun, but I knew it wasn't going to hold until the Navy or Coast Guard or whoever they sent arrived. I tell you, there's a lot to be said for the technology that put us into space in the first place, but when there's no way to power it, it's meaningless. I still don't know why they didn't see fit to give us a good ol' ham radio. Plus, our engineers are good at what they do, but even they couldn't have managed to MacGyver one from what we had.

*MacGyver?*

HY: It's a reference to an old TV show. This super genius with doctorates in a bunch of science stuff, who is also just really savvy, gets himself out of jams by making tools and things out of random parts. I heard that a lot of what he invented was actually legitimately functional, but they intentionally left out steps or pieces so people wouldn't be maiming and killing themselves trying to replicate it. Anyway, we didn't have any of that as an option. It turns out it wasn't necessary though. No sooner had I settled in and prepared myself for a long wait than someone was pointing and shouting at the horizon, telling me there was incoming. I'll be honest, I half expected them to leave us out here to rot. I wouldn't have put it past our military to pull a cover-up like that. Pearce's revelation about the communication shut-out only fed my already heightened mistrust. It will probably come as no surprise, but I am a highly skeptical person. I've seen too much in my years of service to this country to live under delusion.

*Would you call yourself a conspiracy theorist?*

HY: No, but I don't blame a lot of those guys for being highly suspicious of everything. So there they were, our cavalry, and they seemed to be moving at a good clip—a lot faster than I thought those vessels could go. We also heard helos coming in too. It was starting to look like we would get out of there alive after all. Everyone around me was getting overexcited, and I knew I'd better rein them in. I could see the captain two rafts away, looking pretty worse for wear. It wasn't a time to worry about chain of command, so I stepped in and shouted to everyone, "Okay, crew, hang tight. They will be here in no time, but let's do this in an orderly fashion. We'll all get there. Civilian crew first, and then according to rank. You know how to do this. It was in the training manual." Lucas turned to me from the raft floating next to mine and whispered, "That was uncharacteristically fast, don't you think?" I just nodded, not making eye contact. I didn't need him reading anything my face wouldn't hide. He pressed the issue, asking, "So, what do you think? Was it just luck they were close enough?" I told him I thought we shouldn't look a gift horse in the mouth and we just needed to get ready to get out of there. Thankfully, he took the hint. He's a chatty son of a bitch sometimes . . . a lot of times . . . but occasionally common sense prevails with him. Fortunately, this was one of those times.

*So you did think something was off about it.*

HY: Oh, yeah, but that wasn't the time to go down that rabbit hole. The naval ships closed the distance in less than half an hour and moved swiftly to get us on board. It may have seemed like overkill, but I did a final head count to be safe and then signaled the captain that we were all accounted for. Once I had a chance to look beyond our crew, I noticed that there was more than a standard sense of urgency to get us belowdecks and move out. It just added fuel to the fire of suspicion already stoked in my head. But, taking my own advice, I pushed it down and just thanked the heavens that we were on our way home. Another thing I noticed was that what looked to me to be a frigate was hanging back a few hundred yards away. I thought it might have been standard, probably there to protect the operation . . . but it seemed odd. Then, as I was heading belowdecks to check in with my crew and find out where we were headed, I heard someone say, "Not until we're out of the wake zone."

*What did you think that meant? And what is a frigate?*

HY: A frigate is a kind of warship. It's not as big as something like a battle carrier or destroyer, and they usually serve more as escorts for other ships, but they are heavily armed, and pretty fast for a battleship. Anyway, I couldn't begin to guess at that time what it might mean. I was just relieved we were on our way to safety. When I finally located Sonja, she told me we were headed to port in San Diego and would be taken to Miramar for evaluation and debriefing. Made sense. I was sure they wanted to know what the hell happened to us. We weren't going to be a lot of help though. I'm still at a loss for how we pulled off that hat trick.

*Do you think it will remain one of the great mysteries of the universe?*

HY: Possibly. Probably. It's bigger than what my brain can comprehend. So I settled in next to Lucas and he leaned over and muttered under his breath, "Everyone on board that's not us is eyeing us strangely. I get that we were a surprise, but it's not like we are aliens." I reminded him, "Martin, they thought we were dead. It is a lot like seeing a ghost." Sonja advised that we should prepare for reactions like that from everyone. Then she spoke a bit louder so everyone could hear. "Look, everyone, now that we are safely back on terra firma, we need to be preparing ourselves mentally for the reality our family and friends have been living with for probably a few years now—that they'd lost us tragically. It's going to take time for them to adjust. It felt like a bizarre detour to us, but they thought we were gone for good. Our physical reentry was bumpy, but this emotional and mental one is going to be tougher." Every member of the crew nodded and grew somber. It was a grim reminder that things had probably changed a lot. After a few minutes of silence, they began to talk again, imagining how things might be and what they were going to do as soon as they got home—favorite foods to eat, people to hug and kiss, television shows and movies to catch up on. The prospect of all of that lifted their spirits, and I was glad for that. I did my best to show an interest in the brewing excitement, but I had something weighing on me that I couldn't shake, and fortunately, my reputation for being a hard-ass gave me cover to sit with my thoughts.

*So, what was on your mind? Was it the communication blackout or how fast they got to you that had you so bothered?*

HY: Both, and then some. Look, the military has never been known for volunteering information, but they were especially tight-lipped with us. My head was spinning, but once we docked, I thought we would have some answers soon, at least about when we could see our families . . . and get a shower and a decent meal . . . not necessarily in that order. When we disembarked, under guard, though, another thing occurred to me. The whole damn ship was crawling with women.

*I thought you said you didn't have a problem with women in leadership.*

HY: I don't. I'm not opposed to them being around, period. I'm really quite fond of them. And I don't have an objection to them in the military. But it was unusual to have so many aboard a ship. There seemed to be a shocking ratio . . . In fact, there wasn't even a ratio to count. It was all women! I asked one of the deck officers about it as we were lined up to head down the gangway. She just said, "No, sir, it's not unusual." I could tell from her demeanor that I wasn't getting any more than that from her, and the line was moving, so I dropped it . . . but only for the moment. As we got to the bottom, there was a seeming armada of armored, enclosed transport vehicles waiting, along with a veritable platoon of armed guards encircling our passage from ship to shore. Again . . . it appeared to be all female. They loaded us into the vehicles and sped away to our next destination. The rest of the crew sat in silent anticipation, while I sat in silent contemplation. Nothing about this smelled right, and Sonja appeared to be catching up with me. We exchanged looks, but no words, knowing better than to reveal any concern that might trigger a panic. And that's when Awan uttered his first words of the last twenty-four hours. He announced to everyone in earshot, completely inconsiderate of the consequences, "Has anyone else noticed the remarkably high number of females we've encountered?" Of course he would notice. He's Muslim.

*[I start to ask him about that, but he jumps on me before the words can leave my mouth. It seems he is hypersensitive to being accused of having non-politically correct views. It makes me wonder if he hasn't had to go through some sort of sensitivity training.]*

HY: No, I don't mean it like that. I mean, they don't have physical contact with women who aren't family members, so it stands to reason he'd be aware of having to avoid everyone around him. Sonja tried, unsuccessfully, to deflect him off of that course. She said she thought that was an exaggeration and that they were all just happy to see a woman who wasn't her bossing them around. It didn't work. Harris jumped on it and weighed in without any sense that he was stirring a pot of shit stew. "No . . . no, he's right. I don't think I saw a single man on the ship except the ones from our crew." What a time for Harris to actually get a clue. Lucas nudged him with a laugh, asking if he was hoping we'd landed in an Amazonian alternate universe. But I could tell Lucas was wise to the fact that something was off. Harris didn't let it go. He said, "Would that be the worst thing in the world? You may have this Audrey chick to meet, but some of us haven't had a date in way longer than we'd like to think about." I couldn't let them go down this path any longer, so I said, "There will be plenty of time for that after debriefing. Let's focus on what we need to do next, which is attempt to explain how we disappeared into a black hole and came out on the other side of the galaxy." Kamil didn't seem to be satisfied with the lack of response to his observation, but I did provide some distraction for him by turning his mind to the fact that he would get to play with numbers soon. The man really has a one-track mind. I'm kind of amazed he found enough interest in something other than calculations to be able to procreate. Then again, he probably calculated all the passion out of it.

*How long did it take to get to Miramar?*

HY: It was about a forty-five-minute drive. Fifteen minutes after I shut down the conversation, we pulled through the heavily guarded gates of Miramar Base, and, man, was I ready to hit the head and have something to eat, even if it was more government-issued food. If I hadn't been so paranoid about the oddities of the last few hours, I might have been basking in the same fantasy the others had that we were getting some kind of VIP treatment. It felt more clandestine to me, and that had my antennas humming. I thought we might be led to a conference room for debriefing and probably stay in some barracks for a couple of days. But, as we were led underground, I was pretty quickly disabused of that notion.

*Underground, like in some secret facility?*

HY: Well, it looked more like a fallout shelter than an administration area. Enormous metal doors slammed behind us, blocking out every trace of natural light, and fluorescent bulbs flickered to life as we walked down a corridor. When that happened, I could sort of feel the rest of the crew tensing up. They started looking between me and Sonja for clues about how to feel, and I had nothin'. Nothin' but a whole lotta *this ain't right.* Sonja was on deck for the reassurance gig again, because that's not me. We all walked in silence that seemed amplified by the echo of heavy footsteps on concrete. We finally reached what could generously be called a conference room, but felt disturbingly more like a war room. We were "invited" to take a seat and the door closed sharply.

*I bet that set everyone on edge.*

HY: For sure. Chatter erupted immediately, but before we could attempt to address any questions, a group of four people entered and it was like someone just hit the "Mute" button. There was a four-star general and two women in suits, who had that obvious Secret Service look about them. The three of them lined the wall at the end of the room, while a *really* attractive brunette woman, who was probably mid-forties, well-dressed, and carrying an obvious air of authority, stepped to the end of the long conference table and took us all in.

*I'm guessing that was President Marshall. What was it like to meet her?*

HY: She was very formal. She greeted us with something that sounded very scripted. She said, "Ladies and gentlemen, we are very pleased to meet you and have you here safely. I am Margaret Marshall, president of the Americas. I must say, you have thrown us for quite a loop, literally dropping out of the sky on us." Intrigue swept over the room as we took in the news that we now had a female president. I knew we were close with the last election before we left on the mission, but it was still a bit of a shock. Oddly, I was even more surprised by the old brass behind her. He shouldn't have stuck out like a sore thumb, but he was the first man who wasn't part of our team I'd seen since we landed.

*General Stephen Dunne?*

HY: Yes. He looked grizzled and stern, like a general should, but there was something missing . . . Power . . . that's it. Every general I've ever met has made sure you knew they had it in the way they carried themselves, but this guy didn't. The agents flanking him pulled that off more than he did. Things were getting more confusing by the minute. And then it dawned on me . . . She didn't say "President of the United States." And then, just as that thought registered with me, she dropped the big bomb on us.

*I am sure it was beyond comprehension. Before we get into that, let's take a break. I need to check in with my office and we could probably both stand to stretch our legs and take a breather.*

# CHAPTER THREE
## THE NEW WORLD ORDER

*Gentlemen, thank you for agreeing to speak with me. I know our time is short and there is a lot to cover, so let's jump right in and get to it. For the record I am speaking with Dr. Kamil Awan and Sean Flemming of the* Alpha Centauri I *crew. I'd like to start by having you tell us about the day you met the president.*

Kamil Awan (KA): Yes, I would like to speak to that, if you don't mind.

*Sure, Dr. Awan. Go ahead.*

KA: She was courteous and professional, if not entirely forthcoming. It was quite something to see a woman at the pinnacle of leadership. Though I served under a very capable female captain, I did not honestly expect to see a female president in my lifetime.

*Why is that?*

KA: I did not think the country could come together on such a progressive move. Though, I suppose, it wasn't really in my lifetime.

*I guess that is true. So, what did she tell you when you met with her?*

KA: Well, it was clear from the beginning that she was not happy to be in front of us and did not look forward to saying what she had to say. She talked around issues quite a bit through the first half hour or so, while telling us she recognized we were anxious to know what had been happening and to reconnect with our loved ones.

*You had a family you left behind, correct? One of the few crew members with children?*

KA: I believe I was the only one with children. The decision to go was not easy, but it was necessary. When she told us they couldn't allow us to communicate with anyone at that time, it was not well received. We were all outraged. How could they deny us this after all we'd been through? It was not fair. But we could not focus on that, as there were so many things we needed to know, and we had been told we would not have an audience with her for long. She asked us to hold our questions until she had finished because there was a lot to explain, a lot to decide, and it wasn't all going to happen at once.

*Sean, what about you? How did you feel about hearing you couldn't reach out to family and friends?*

Sean Flemming (SF): Well, I guess my situation was a little different from Dr. Awan's. My twin sister, Natalie, was also part of the crew, so I had my family with me. See, we grew up in foster care and didn't really have a lot of friends because we were moved around a lot. We just had each other, but at least they always kept us together. She was always a lot smarter than me, so she went to school and got a medical assistant degree. I just worked in a restaurant. But she found out about this whole opportunity through Ms. Sarah, who was her advisor at school, and she got us both in. I guess we were good candidates because we didn't have a lot of ties to home and were fine with leaving for so long. Anyway, Natalie applied for both of us and got me a job in the galley, since I have experience with that, and she got onto Dr. Tilden's team.

*So you weren't bothered by the secrecy?*

SF: Oh, I don't know about that. It bugged me, but I guess I was just okay with waiting a bit and giving them a chance to adjust to us dropping in out of nowhere. I didn't have a bug up my a . . . um, sorry. I have to watch my kitchen language. I just wasn't feeling as rushed as some of the others. Also I kinda felt sorry for the president. I mean, I wouldn't have wanted to be in her shoes.

*I guess her job there definitely wasn't enviable. Dr. Awan, what was your reaction?*

KA: I was rather impatient, but I did feel for President Marshall as well. I certainly would not have wanted to be the bearer of such bad news, and to have to tell us there was even more we couldn't know due to national security issues. It must have been difficult to walk the line between satisfying our need to know with what we weren't cleared to know.

*That is very understanding of you both.*

KA: You have to remember, we are accustomed to the way government agencies operate. We may not always like it, but we adapt to serve the whole. Of course it helped having a leader like Captain Halverson, who never asked anything of us she wasn't willing to do herself. A fine example of a leader.

*Yes, from what I understand, you all served your countries bravely, and we are in your debt for the risks you took to further space exploration, and Captain Halverson, in particular, did the team proud, bringing you through unimaginable peril.*

KA: Yes, she did. She insisted on being there for the debriefing, but I know we were all concerned about her health and feared she may not have received the level of medical care necessary for her injury. She said Dr. Tilden gave her a thorough going-over, and I know he is a fine physician, but he was not able to do any kinds of scans. However, she was in charge, so we did not press the issue with her. We all just wanted to know what was going on.

*You said the president hedged a good bit initially. What did you learn from her?*

KA: Once we were settled down, she finally said, "There's no easy way to say this, especially considering how hard you fought to get back home. But . . . home is not what you remember. In fact, I dare say, many of you may not be going home at all."

*Well, that still sounds like a nonanswer.*

SF: Right? I told Natalie the same thing. And Commander Young . . . Hunter . . . you know him?

*Yes, I am acquainted.*

SF: So you know what he's like. Well, he said that too, only he wasn't so polite as you about it . . . and with the president. I tell you, that guy has a set of brass . . . sorry. I promise I'll watch that. I'm just used to being around a bunch of guys in a hot, messy kitchen, where that kind of talk is how you get by. Anyway, I think he made an impression on her. I don't think she was used to having people pop off at her like that. To be honest, I think she kinda liked it.

*How did she respond to him?*

SF: She sorta smiled and then got real serious again and tried to get control of the room, but I think she really wants him on her side.

*Dr. Awan, you know Commander Young fairly well. Do you think he is likely to acquiesce to her?*

KA: Hunter doesn't hold back his opinions, and he is prone to cutting you off to get those opinions across. So, no, I don't believe he is, but

President Marshall did try. At one point she said she would explain, but in order to get through this, she needed all of us to refrain from interrupting. She assured us we would get to all of our questions, and she would probably address some we didn't know to ask. It seemed like she was still stalling . . . almost as if she were trying to find the nerve to tell us the truth. Doing hard things is part of that job, but I don't think any president has faced the kinds of challenges this one has.

*It's fair to say there probably haven't been any more trying times in the history of our world. There isn't much that would rival it in scope and scale of tragedy, that's for sure.*

KA: She finally began the process of bringing us up to date on all that had transpired since we left, starting with the fact that we went off radar approximately six months into our mission, in 2025.

SF: Which was pretty lame, in my opinion. Like we didn't know this already. And everybody let her know it too.

KA: Yes, but she was going somewhere with it. She then told us we had not reentered from wherever we went in the same year. Commander Young asked if it was 2027 or 2028.

*So, how did you react when she told you it was 2065?*

KA: I would say the best description is stunned silence.

*No gasps and shrieks . . . no hand-wringing, wailing, gnashing of teeth?*

KA: You have to remember, we had just come out of a literal black hole—something you are not supposed to survive. This was yet another incomprehensible detail. It was going to take time to sink in. At any rate the silence was deafening. I think we were just waiting for something else to happen, to have this all make sense.

SF: Yeah, I was half expecting her to say "Just kidding!" or that I'd wake up and find out all of this had been a horrible nightmare, except I hadn't been drinking or anything, so it was totally real.

*Maybe surreal?*

SF: Yeah, she said one of the reasons they needed to keep us there was because they had to download a ton of information to us, and also had to get intel from us on everything before we could even consider going back to "normal life" . . . whatever that means. So, not only were we stuck there, we were about to get interrogated.

*So, what was the plan? How long did they expect to keep you locked down?*

KA: She said she honestly couldn't predict at that point. She had a great deal to cover on how the world had changed—about what had happened over the last forty years—and how all of it was going to impact what happened next for them. She said we would understand, once we had all the information. There was only one aspect of this new world that interested me at that moment, so I asked, "Do we even still have families? What do they know of our return?" She said no one knew we were here yet, with the exception of the NASA crew that helped us land and the retrieval team that brought us to the site.

*That must have been a shock for everyone.*

KA: Yes, some took it better than others.

SF: It really sucked for Lucas.

*Why is that?*

SF: Dude, he just sounded so betrayed by God, life, the government . . . everything. He was like, "So . . . that wasn't Audrey? I wasn't talking to Audrey at Ground Control?" The pres said she figured this Audrey person had retired by now. She told him he had been talking to another chick named Amelia. She worked in Pasadena, where the Audrey lady worked when we left.

*That is an uncanny coincidence.*

KA: Yes, indeed. Amelia worked in the in Space Flight Operations Facility. When we launched our mission, it was a full-scale operation, but we were told they do little there at this point. She had detected our reentry a few days prior. She began tracking our movements, but assumed it was a meteor at first, then thought it might just be a disabled satellite.

*That was until Lucas made contact, right? I guess he had been imagining a special homecoming with Audrey. I talked to Amelia. She said she had been asked to pretend to be Audrey. This must have been the first he was learning of it. That seems pretty cruel, I have to say.*

KA: I can't imagine this was how President Marshall would have wanted to handle delivering this kind of news, but I doubt she knew. There was nothing easy about any of what she was telling us. Nothing like this had ever happened before, so there certainly was no playbook to guide them.

*It was an unfortunate series of events to be sure. How did the others react?*

KA: As I'm sure you can guess, Commander Young erupted with a few choice words. He said he knew there was something "shady" going on. Officer Pearce Johnson had shared with him that our comms were cut while we were still coming in. He surmised that we had not lost communication when we hit the surface. He accused the president of ordering them to cut us off. His assumption was that this was so no one would detect our signal.

*Were you aware of that?*

KA: No, I was in engineering. Pearce was in the communications bay. We don't have access to the same data.

*Oh, of course. Well, was he right? Did they cut communication?*

KA: President Marshall assured us that if that is what happened, it wasn't an order that came from her. She said it was far more likely that the ship lost communication as a result of the damage sustained coming through the atmosphere as it did. It could have been a bandwidth disruption. We were out at sea, after all, and the types of transmission waves we were using were not exactly stable in those zones.

*Is that what* you *think happened?*

KA: I don't know. It doesn't make sense to me, knowing what I know about the design of the ship and the technology we were operating. But I also don't know what they were working with on the ground at that point. I guess we'll never know.

*It remains a mystery?*

KA: It would seem so, but Hunter wasn't finished. He continued his tirade on his suspicions over how fast they got to us. I was simply grateful we weren't adrift in the ocean any longer than necessary. But, for him, it was suspect that it didn't take the three hours Lucas had estimated. Maybe there's something to that as well, but I will leave it to him to explore.

*Did Hunter accept her explanation?*

SF: Seriously? *Hunter?* No way, man. He was going on about the warship he saw that stayed behind after they picked us up, and then he wanted to know what was up with all the women. He pushed hard, calling it "cloak-and-dagger bullshit." That's when she said all of that had to do with stuff she needed to tell us and she might actually get to do that if he'd stop interrupting. Like I said, there is some fiery chemistry between those two. I wouldn't be surprised if they hook up.

KA: Sean, remember, that's the president you are referring to.

SF: Sure, but she's a woman too.

KA: Still, a little respect, please. When Hunter stopped ranting, she told us in a nutshell that America . . . the world . . . was a very different place from the one we left, and we would get the information we needed in as clear and concise a way as possible if we would just work with her a bit.

*Seems like a fair enough request. How did she proceed?*

KA: Well, I don't think it went as she planned. Sarah Tilden chimed in with a question we all wanted to ask, which was whether we were going to be able to retrieve our personal belongings from the ship. She pointed out that we all had mementos we took with us, since we were going to be away from our families for a long time. With so much having changed, she feared those might be all we had left. That's when President Marshall told us our ship had been destroyed.

*So, then, Hunter's speculation was on point.*

KA: Yes, and he let her know he knew it. He shouted that he had figured out that armed ship wasn't there for protection. Captain Halverson tried to calm him, asking him what getting angry was going to change at that point. She reminded him that his disruptions were only keeping us from finding out what we needed to know. She asked him to give the president the respect she was due.

SF: Yeah, and she told him to shut the hell up.

*She was very effective at reining him in. Wasn't she?*

KA: Yes, Hunter always deferred to her. It just shows you what an effective leader she was. He was still enraged, but settled back in his seat. Still, I have to give credit to President Marshall. She admitted he was right. She explained it was necessary to destroy the ship because they didn't know what had happened to us, what we could have brought back with us—radiation, cosmic debris, whatever—that could be toxic to this planet's environment.

*That didn't sound like a stretch to you?*

SF: It sure as hell did to me, but what do I know? I'm just a cook.

KA: Well, it wasn't entirely out of the realm of possibility. We couldn't even speculate as to where we had been during those forty years, only that time basically stood still for us. I believe it will be years of research and observation before we know the impacts that may have had on us.

*How did that happen anyway?*

KA: Without being too technical, there is something that happens when you approach the speed of light called time dilation.

*Yeah, I've read a little about that in doing my homework for this project.*

KA: Well, because of the physics involved, time basically slows down for the traveler. What you experience as five years would be less than three for someone traveling at the rate we were. However, from what we can discern, we accelerated from the 85 percent capacity we had to nearly 99 percent of the speed of light as we approached the event horizon—the edge of the black hole. The gravitational pull gave us that extra boost. We weren't just speeding through space those forty years. We were in another dimension of space—accessed through what we think was a wormhole—which is why we didn't really age.

SF: So we were, like, in an alternate reality or something?

KA: I'm not sure I would use those words. Perhaps more of a state of suspended animation. Either way, we definitely were experiencing something we as humans have never encountered before and don't yet have the capacity to understand.

*Do you think we will ever figure it out?*

KA: Hard to say. I think we could get there someday. But from what we learned about the state of the world now, I'm not sure that will happen.

*Yeah, okay, so let's get back to that. What did you learn?*

KA: President Marshall tried to continue, explaining that there were many unknowns and they didn't have a clue how to integrate us into this new world. She said we presented a massive disruption to things we couldn't begin to comprehend yet. And, because of that, there couldn't be any trace of our presence until they figured out a few things. At that point we were still stuck on the destruction of the ship. It was truly inconceivable. That's when Michael . . . Dr. Michael Li . . . said that as a scientist his priorities might be a little different from others, but he couldn't get past the fact that they had just erased not only our existence, but a whole lot of data we could use for future exploration. I agreed with him. That is when she told us the space program was all but dismantled some time ago, and there would be no galactic exploration for the foreseeable future.

*Ah, so that's what you were referring to. That must have been devastating news for all of you.*

KA: Most certainly. We could not comprehend such a thing. After all, this is what we had devoted our lives to and sacrificed for. Then she explained that there was an even greater reason for destroying the ship. You may know that the *Alpha Centauri* was powered by a biofuel created for the aeronautics program from a highly specialized, genetically modified strain of corn called APOLLO-VI-24.

*Right. It was a super strain that took years to perfect, but made your trip possible. It was problematic in some other ways, but I'm not sure what that has to do with destroying a multimillion-dollar spacecraft.*

KA: Well, it turns out that biofuel—or, more precisely, the corn it came from—was believed to be the solution to far more than a sustainable rocket fuel.

*So she told you about that?*

KA: Yes, it's such a shame. I was not involved in the creation of the fuel; that was the job of chemists and bioengineers. However, I was a part of the team that developed the engines that could be powered by it. It truly was a brilliant innovation because biofuel isn't as flammable and could be carried on board to fuel our return trip. It seems another group of scientists who came along after we left believed it could do much more. They found that this crop was even more special than originally thought. It had a shorter gestation time—approximately fifty-three days instead of the standard sixty-five-and it was hardy in all climate zones. Additionally, it proved to be perennial, and self-propagated like a weed.

*Yes, that is where the whole mess got started. But it still doesn't explain why they decided to wipe out your ship.*

SF: Yeah, I never quite got that either.

KA: She was working her way toward that, but had to explain why the corn was a problem first. See, at the time they discovered what this corn could do, there was an alarming uptick in famine in heavily populated, less-developed regions—areas like my home country, Pakistan. The devolving climate crisis had been a big problem for some time. It was part of why we were going to Proxima b in the first place. We were looking for options in case we ruined this planet. Apparently, it got worse, because they were in dire need for a sustainable, durable food source. Many felt this corn would provide a solution for a perceived threat to the very existence of humanity. Though she did not explain how they got this, when GMOs were banned from the food supply in many countries.

*The prohibitions of GMOs existing when you left the planet had been lifted in most regions due to the famine. It was a process and part of the resistance was actually from the GMO corporations. They couldn't get the patent on it because it was held by the US government and they wouldn't sell.*

KA: That would make sense. However, they really should have known, just as with all other genetically modified products, that would be too good to be true. There were plenty of experiments gone awry for them to learn from—cloning animals in China, among other things. Then again, desperation does seem to make people do desperate things.

*I'd say, sometimes it's ego that makes us do desperate things.*

KA: Yes, I think that's fair to say. President Marshall, though, insisted this was out of self-preservation. They began by farming it in the plains areas in the US and distributed it to poverty-stricken areas like Africa, India, and Russia. The Americans felt they were the best equipped for turning it into food sources that could make a difference. This is when she told us of the dire unforeseen consequences.

*That was a lot for you all to absorb at once.*

KA: Yes, it was. I think we were all reaching a saturation point when Hunter spoke up and said that as much as he wanted to know what was going on, we hadn't eaten in quite a long time, and we really needed some fuel to keep going in what he expected to be a much longer conversation. The general . . . Dunne . . . stuck his head out the door and spoke to someone outside to take care of that.

*There was still some really important information she hadn't gotten to, right?*

SF: Yeah, probably the most important part of the story. President Marshall disappeared when the topic of food came up. I guess she saw that as her cue to bail.

KA: Although we needed to eat, we were becoming really impatient. However, if we had known what was coming, we probably would have chosen to remain in blissful ignorance a bit longer.

*That's probably true, but isn't there something to just ripping off the Band-Aid?*

KA: That would have been my preference, to be sure. But that is not how things unfolded.

*Well, how did they . . . unfold?*

KA: They brought food in for us about twenty minutes later and we sat clustered in groups, many of us whispering among ourselves, some just hugging and consoling each other. A few just sat alone, staring blankly, mindlessly shoving food into their mouths. We were nearly finished when President Marshall came back in. I think we all turned to her with expectation and desperation.

SF: She started in with some meaningless crap about how she hoped our meals were an improvement over the powdered and packaged stuff we'd been stuck with. Being one of the guys who worked hard to provide decent food for the crew, I found that pretty offensive.

*I can see why. I'm sure she didn't mean it that way though. Just a poor attempt at an icebreaker.*

KA: I took that opportunity to bring up something I noticed. As someone who must be mindful of my diet, for what I imagine are obvious reasons, I pay close attention to what is provided in group settings. I'd never had so many options in a catered meal without making a special request. She seemed annoyed by my observation and thanked me somewhat patronizingly. I suppose she was trying to move on, but I said she didn't understand what I meant. You see, there was no meat, and nothing with any corn or corn by-products. I wanted to know why, if the super corn was turned into a food source, it wasn't what they served us. A few people rolled their eyes. I know it's not the first time I have complained about food selection, but it is something I have to deal with for every meal. And, truth be told, I was not off base at all in noting the conspicuous absence. President Marshall said it actually was quite relevant. The most impoverished nations at the time were the first to receive the APOLLO corn—famine-stricken parts of Africa, India, and Russia—which led to even regions such as the European countries that had banned GMOs to open themselves up to receiving it.

*Yes, for the first two to three years, it seemed like they had been granted a miracle. Economies were stabilizing, prosperity was spreading across the globe, and opportunity was becoming available to everyone, but it unraveled pretty quickly.*

KA: It does seem they made quite the mess of things. I can see how it would have been initially perceived as a great solution for everyone; but, if I understand correctly, international corporations soon wanted in on the action, and greed took over.

*Yeah, the US kept production at home and guarded it closely, supposedly to prevent it from falling into the hands of those who could corrupt it. Clearly, that didn't work. Like most natural resources, such as oil, it became the fuel behind major global conflict. War broke out. It didn't last long, a little over three months, but it went nuclear—not in the apocalyptic-wasteland way you see in movies, and not* literally *nuclear, but close. China deployed bioweapons.*

SF: I still don't know how they let it get that far. I thought everyone was sane enough to keep the lid on that stuff.

KA: They used dirty bombs to destroy our supply of corn and contaminate the area against any future planting, in the hopes of making it necessary to plant elsewhere, opening up their access to it. The world lost millions of people as various regions fought over control. This eclipsed the casualties of both prior World Wars, not only in ground warfare, but also in bombings and widespread desolation.

*Yes, the reason we don't have the continental and country designations that existed when you left us, and are now aggregated into five regions, is because significant parts of the world were rendered uninhabitable for several decades, and our global population was a fraction of what it was. But that wasn't the only reason for the population decline.*

KA: That was the truly shocking part. The corn itself had an unimaginable impact, starting slowly, virtually imperceptibly, she said.

*It wasn't until the census in 2030 that the reports revealed population growth had not only undershot projections based on the increased food supply, they even missed the mark on estimations from previous tables. We saw about a 30 percent decline in what they had expected to see. The world's population had fallen below 6 billion—the lowest it had been since the turn of the 19th Century. Most of us lived through this crisis . . . this pandemic . . . and it became sort of normal for us, but for you it must have been mind-blowing.*

KA: Yes, for a genetically altering plague to be spread through the world's population through the food supply. If the impact weren't so even-handed, one might suspect a conspiracy.

SF: It sure as hell blew my mind. I mean, even though we were in this zone of expecting to be around only the same twenty-six people for several years, we still had in the back of our heads that there was this whole planet of people back home waiting for us to come back. And now billions of them were just . . . *poof* . . . gone! That messes with your head big-time.

*I can only imagine.*

KA: It isn't unusual for some regions of the world to see dramatic swings in population numbers in either direction over decades. President Marshall explained that they did not understand the source of the decline initially because the increase in deaths had been attributed to the war. Eventually they launched a study to assess what actually was happening. Dr. Tilden was the first to pick up on it. He jumped in, saying, "Births. You saw a decline in births as well, correct?" She said he was definitely in the ballpark, but not entirely accurate. She pointed to the studies we had from the last century that had shown a general decline in family size. Families had fewer children when the culture shifted away from being agrarian-based. And even before 2020 there were studies showing how the generation known as Millennials was waiting until much later in life to have children, if they did at all. The study, which they did, found that the notable decline was specifically in male births. Have you ever heard a theory about male births increasing around wartime?

*No. Is that real?*

KA: I don't really know, but Sarah Tilden suggested there is a centuries-old theory that nature has a way of balancing out sex ratios. Wars come in cycles—generations—and more males are born in the wake of a war, in theory, so nature can . . . for lack of a better term . . . restock the supply for the next round. Some people laughed at her, but I don't know. There is some logic to it.

SF: Yeah, I still don't know about that. It seemed pretty far out to me, but she sounded really sure about it, and she is such a great lady . . . been so good to me and Natalie. I definitely didn't want to make fun of her.

KA: As far as I know, they've never *scientifically* proven the reason behind it, but it would seem there are numbers to support the theory all the same. Who knows? Regardless, it took another couple of years before they finally linked the decline to a reproductive issue stemming from what basically amounted to a virus that altered the human DNA. Apparently, the Y chromosome was no longer available—in other words, no more male children. That's when she told us there have been no boys born since 2035. The room was probably the most silent it had been.

SF: Yeah, except for the sound of a bunch of jaws hitting the floor.

*That wasn't the whole calculation though.*

KA: No, she explained the other contributing factors—how they discovered there was an increase in male deaths not related to the war. As the "virus" spread and took hold, they found there had been a surge in Y-chromosome and male-dominant diseases, such as prostate cancer and heart disease, Parkinson's, ALS, and some other cancers. They missed those initially because, with the exception of heart disease, most of those can be long, drawn-out illnesses, or at least take some time to be symptomatic. Also, the genetic alterations weakened the immune systems of every human, not just the men.

*That is why it took a few years for them to isolate the cause of the epidemic and eradicate that strain of corn. That meant any area where the corn had been planted—and it was everywhere—had to be burned so there would be no trace left of the species.*

SF: Dr. Awan, I still don't get how they managed to have male babies for a few years after everything happened. If the corn did that to the chromosome, how did that work?

*That's a good question, Sean. I still haven't been able to fully understand that.*

KA: Please note, my area of expertise is not in this type of science. However, the first thing you need to know is that the sex of a child is determined by the father. And, since it took a while before everyone was impacted by the disease, as long as the man didn't have the mutation, he could produce a male child. It wasn't until everyone was infected that this abnormality was activated in all men. Also, they were apparently able to sustain the reproductive ratio for a bit longer after that by utilizing genetic material that had been donated and stored.

SF: What, like sperm banks?

KA: Well, yes. Exactly. I just find that to be a crude term.

SF: Sorry. I'm trying to get better about that.
KA: It's fine, Sean. Unfortunately, it seems within five years, they had depleted the supply in the banks and, obviously, couldn't refill it. President Marshall said they had the world's best scientists collaborating for a solution and they found a way to immunize the existing population, but never did find a cure.

*I've never really understood, what good is an immunization if it doesn't fix anything?*

KA: You're not wrong. It does feel kind of pointless, looking at it from a short-term perspective. I assume, they were hoping that if they could arrest the spread of it, they would have time to find a cure. You see, even though the problem most directly affected men, a woman could be a carrier and pass it along to a male child who had not consumed the corn. Although, as far as I know, they have yet to figure out how to turn the Y chromosome back on. If they can accomplish that, the immunization of everyone will prevent female carriers from undoing that work.

*It still baffles me that scientists would mess with something like this, knowing what a disaster it was to play with the genes of animals, like they did.*

KA: Yes, the scientific community should have come under a lot of fire for that. For as long as there has been experimentation, there has also been the question "Just because we can, does it mean we should?" The only thing I can figure is that those previous disasters were the results of altering the DNA of an animal, and this was a plant that already had a variety of genetic modifications performed for decades; so something like this must not have been on their radar.

*Thank you for explaining that. This makes sense to me, though I'm not sure I hold the same hope for a solution. But now that you are back, maybe that can change. Was this all she told you?*

KA: Well, it wasn't everything we needed to know, but at that point she handed off to Major Lydia Statham. President Marshall explained the major would stay behind to continue debriefing us and bringing us up to speed. She said we would need to undergo a battery of tests to assess our health and receive immunization updates as well. We asked if we would be getting the vaccine as well. She said it was definitely protocol. They couldn't risk exposure since we had not been inoculated . . . and, as you said, now that we had returned, they thought we might be able to help them find a cure. She thanked us for our patience in the process and admitted it was going to take some time to figure out how to proceed. Then she promised to make sure we were as comfortable and accommodated as possible.

SF: Before she left, she came down hard on us, telling us not to even try to reach out to anyone outside. It felt like an order, like a law or something. Like we might go to Leavenworth if we did.

*Probably just a scare tactic, but better you didn't try.*

KA: Before she could leave, Hunter got in one last question. He asked, "When you were introduced, they said president of the *Americas*, not the United States. Is that because of what you said about not having the same countries and continents we remember? Is the United States still a thing?" She didn't answer. She passed that off to Major Statham.

*Typical politician. I guess some things never change. Thank you both for your time. You have provided valuable information. I hope the rest of your transition back into real life goes more smoothly than the first few hours did.*

# CHAPTER FOUR
## OF LAB MICE AND MEN

Abraham Tilden (AT): If I could, before we go any further, I would like to go on record as saying I believe the team at the holding facility was professional and courteous, and they did the very best they could under unimaginable circumstances. I hold no ill will toward anyone, save a few bad actors.

*Thank you, Dr. Tilden. Duly noted. Are you willing to go on record about the rest of your experience?*

AT: Yes, I will do my best to relate events, as I recall them, though I am not a spring chicken, so we may have to do this in installments.

*Yes, sir. I will accommodate your needs, and go according to your pace, but I will be thorough.*

AT: Fair enough. Where should we start?

*Why don't you pick up with what happened after President Marshall spoke with you all? I'd especially like to hear your professional opinion on the examinations and other procedures you were subjected to at the medical facility.*

AT: Well, we were delivered quite a blow in that briefing. Our heads were spinning, trying to process everything we learned. And here we thought *we* were going to be the biggest surprise that day. Major Statham—Lydia—took over when President Marshall left and she was firm, but gracious. She asked us to remember it would be far more effective to do this in as orderly and methodical a way as possible, or we would just end up even more confused than we already were. The poor young woman seemed really overwhelmed, and I could not say I blamed her. The questions, accusations, and demands were coming at her rapid-fire. I was not an officer on the crew, but I was the oldest member of the team and considered myself as a sort of patriarch, if you will. And they treated me as such, most of the time. I decided I should probably try to wrangle them to help her out. Captain Halverson was a strong and capable leader, but the blow to her head was worse than she wanted anyone to know, and I did not think she had the capacity at the time to keep everyone in line.

Hunter was definitely serving as more of an alarmist than a comforting force, so I found myself rising from my seat and attempting to speak over the din of grumbling without having to shout. I really am not fond of raising my voice, but it seemed to be what was required. I spoke as loudly as I could, pleading, "Okay, okay, okay! Everyone! Just calm down. We need to give the major the room to address each of these, one at a time. We all need information and all have different priorities around what we think needs to be answered first. We are a team, so we should act like it rather than pushing personal agendas." Hunter's response was not especially helpful. He asked, how were we supposed to sit back and wait for them to dole out information as they saw fit? He said, "We all know how the government operates."

Do you see what I mean? Hunter is a wonderful man and sharp as a tack, but when his hackles are raised, he loses his tenuous grip on his ability to read the room and does not seem to care if he is inflammatory. I told him we do not know anything about anything anymore and asked him to give the woman a chance. I was sympathetic though. I knew I was in better stead than the others; I had my bride with me, and we did not have any children to worry about. The sense of loss was somewhat lessened for me. Still, we had lives and friends and other family members, and this was deeply alarming for us too. All the same I knew I needed to tread carefully and consider all the other pieces of what they were feeling.

*It is obvious why you were considered the patriarch of the group. But, with tempers flaring, it must have been difficult to keep everyone calm.*

AT: Yes, and had Major Statham not taken that moment to round us up and move us to our housing facility to get settled in and be processed, I fear it likely would have bubbled over.

*"Processed." That doesn't sound like an especially comforting term.*

AT: It was not. I wanted to believe it was not as bad as it sounded, but I felt the need for clarification and had to ask in the calmest way possible so the others did not take cues from my tone. The major explained we would need IDs, blood work, immunizations, and an overall physical evaluation. She said we would also get a change of clothes, toiletries, and linens.

*It's hard for that* not *to sound like prison. Were there any red flags for you in this?*

AT: I cannot say it triggered anything for me in that moment. These seemed like reasonable things for them to do for us. We certainly would need current IDs, and the medical evaluations would be standard at the completion of any type of mission, but especially given the anomalous experience we had. Hunter, however, was true to form and equated it to prison as well. He loves to poke the bear and was gearing up to be the biggest thorn in everyone's side. I never sensed that he resented female authority; he served under Captain Halverson admirably. However, he is not one to suffer fools gladly, and he definitely does not like being kept in the dark . . . about *anything*. He is accustomed to bureaucratic processes, but this expedition seemed to have given him license to step out of line with authority and chain of command in a way that really surprised me. Thankfully, Major Statham chose to ignore him and began herding us out the door and down a labyrinth of corridors, which, as I said, was a good move on her part to distract Hunter and defuse the powder keg.

When we reached a massive steel-reinforced door, she leaned down to a panel mounted in the wall to the side for a retinal scan. This type of high-tech security was just coming into commercial use when we left the planet, but was still very much the stuff of spy movies for most. One would think such safety measures would be reassuring, giving us the sense of being protected. But seeing that, I had to agree with Hunter, it felt more like incarceration—keeping us *in*, instead of others *out*. The heavy door groaned into motion and slid into a pocket in the wall to the left, clanging as it came to a stop. We stepped through the threshold into a bright, sterile environment lit with fluorescent bulbs and smelling of industrial-grade cleaner. In short, it was a lab. Something all too familiar to me. It should have been comforting to be in my native environment, but all of a sudden I was gaining an increasing understanding of how lab mice felt. Once we were all gathered close to her, Major Statham told us there were units prepared for each of us designated with our names on each door. She said the women would find their quarters down the corridor to the left and men would find theirs to the right. Sarah asked her about our accommodations and she said she was sorry, but we would have separate quarters for the time being.

My lovely wife is kind, sensitive, and tenderhearted, but also very set in her ways regarding certain things. She asked why, when we are married, would we have to be separated. You see, we hadn't spent a night apart since this whole ordeal began. I give Major Statham credit. She sounded very sympathetic, saying she understood that it seemed unreasonable, but explained it was necessary as they did our evaluations and ran tests. Sarah was not satisfied with that, so I had to pull her aside. No one needed her stirring up more outrage and anxiety. If she got hysterical, it would set everyone off. I said, "Sarah, hon, it will be okay. We should not make this harder on anyone than it has to be." She insisted that they sure were not trying to avoid making things hard on us.

While I saw her point, it was not the time to make a scene. I reminded her that none of the others had their spouses or partners with them. In fact . . . and I was almost hesitant to even say this out loud, and I lowered my voice even more as I said, ". . . they may not ever see their loved ones again. Can we not be considerate of their situation? Would you please do that for me?" She begrudgingly conceded, but made sure I knew it was for me, not for those, as she put it, "holding us captive."

*Sounds like everyone was beginning to show signs of the ordeal wearing on them.*

AT: Most assuredly. We shuffled down the hall searching for our names on the placards. They had us housed two or three to a bay. The younger men of the crew seem bewildered and the older ones, knowingly troubled. Harris was one of the first to voice his concerns, asking how they managed to put this together so quickly when we had only been there a few hours. Hunter snapped at him, calling him naïve. He suggested this place had obviously been around for a long time. He called it a secret government-testing site for who knows what, speculating that all sorts of unscrupulous experiments were performed there.

*Do you think that's true?*

AT: I honestly cannot say. Hunter is more inclined to that way of thinking than I am; however, recent events certainly set a mind to wondering. That said, I felt he really needed to dial it back. As a leader his behavior was unbecoming. I understood that this whole situation had him really triggered, stoking his fires of mistrust, but this was hard enough without his inflaming irrational fears as well. I asked him to keep it to himself . . . or come to me privately until we knew the whole picture. He was in a state, ranting about how none of this was okay, and he was sure we would not get answers without knocking down some doors and demanding them.

*He wasn't wrong, was he?*

AT: Well, no, and as he said, they were not going to volunteer information if they could avoid it, but we needed to be strategic about this. I reminded him that the more he raised a ruckus, the more tight-lipped they would be. They would quickly decide they could not trust us with more information if we were being antagonistic. It was not a situation either of us liked, but there was little we could do about it at the time. I put my arm around him and guided him to our quarters, trying to calm him as we moved into this strange environment, which would be our new home for the foreseeable future.

*So you moved from one confined space to another without really seeing the outside world.*

AT: Yes, that is true, unless you count the surprisingly short amount of time we spent floating at sea and the drive from the dock to the base. We went from small cabins on the *Alpha Centauri* to . . . well, I cannot think of a better word than *cubicle*, but I suppose there was some comfort in the familiarity. Once we settled in, I told Hunter I thought the best course of action was to toe the line, take it all in, and then debrief each night in private, out of earshot of the others. Then we could use our shared brainpower to try to piece together what they told us with what we observed, and maybe get a more accurate picture of what was really going on.

*You didn't think they had the place wired?*

AT: Oh, I was quite sure they did, and I knew we would have to be creative. But for the moment I felt the wisest thing for us to do was take advantage of the few moments of downtime to rest for a bit until they reconvened a meeting with us. I needed him to have his wits about him.

*They started running tests on you immediately, right?*

AT: Almost. They allowed us about two hours to ourselves before it started. I was just getting comfortable when a voice boomed over the loudspeaker calling us together in the lab, terse and formal, but still sounding young . . . and female. Hunter was spot-on in his observation. It seemed that not only had the male population diminished significantly, the women were in charge of everything. That was a lot to ponder. Women were beginning to occupy more positions of power when we left, and there were lots of projections of how that would change things. I was very curious to see if those predictions were right. Imagine—a world run by women. What must that be like? More peaceful? Healthier? Softer? More nature-oriented? I had so many questions!

*Well, Dr. Tilden, I don't have to imagine it. It is the world I've spent most of my life in. You'll come to find out it is a mixed blessing.*

AT: I hope I have the chance to find out. In the meantime . . . I had to rouse Hunter so we could head down to the meeting space. I had the distinct impression that they would not tolerate lollygagging. He grumbled as he pulled himself to an upright position. He had dropped into a deep sleep almost as soon as his head hit the pillow. It would seem he determined fighting it was a futile exercise. I had not been able to sleep, so I went to check on Sarah. I found her resting and did not want to disturb her, so I came back to my bunk and just replayed the events since we came back in contact with our home planet. I found myself joining Hunter in his frustration and outrage over how we had been treated. It definitely was a good thing he got some rest, so his temper was a little more manageable. As we left our quarters, he made it clear the nap did not do much to take the edge off. He whispered to me, "Abe, it's only my curiosity that is overriding my resistance to being summoned."

I headed out into the hallway to make sure the others were responding to the call as well. It seemed as though most of the crew wisely took the opportunity to get some much-needed rest—either that, or they just collapsed from sheer exhaustion, once the adrenaline subsided. It was hard to believe we had been back on the planet for less than half a day at that point. In some ways it felt like a lifetime ago that we reentered our solar system through the wormhole or whatever spat us out of the unknown darkness. But the download of life-altering information we were expected to absorb since then felt like a whirlwind of madness. Once we knew we were headed home, we had no idea how everyone on Earth would react to our reappearance, though we expected them to be surprised. Never would we have anticipated they would have an even more inconceivable curveball for us.

*I think there was plenty of shock to go around. How did the testing go?*

AT: When we got there, Major Statham stood at the ready, not masking her impatience. We gathered around her, certainly more haphazardly than the military formation she was obviously accustomed to seeing. She greeted us rather stoically, saying, "Hello, everyone, I trust you found your quarters sufficient and were able to get a little rest. We still have a few hours ahead of us before you can settle in for the evening." That garnered an uninhibited response of frustration from probably half the crew in unison, with varying degrees of aggravation, but all revealing their breaking point was approaching. The major shouted over us by saying they would move this along as swiftly as possible, but she needed our cooperation to make that happen. Getting through this part with order and precision would allow us to gather what we needed so we could turn in early. The muttered complaints and groans of frustration rumbled through the room, but everyone seemed ready to acquiesce . . . with, perhaps, the exception of Hunter.

*He was spoiling for a fight?*

AT: I certainly thought one was coming, though I had hoped we were on the same page after our heart-to-heart. Major Statham also was a bit wary as she asked him what he needed when he interrupted her, yet again. He surprised me by asking if it would be helpful to group us by age, rank, gender, or some other demographic to facilitate the process. It was so unexpected that I wondered what he was up to. I was not fool enough to think he had all of a sudden seen the light and become a company man. Major Statham, however, seemed grateful and seized on the suggestion, telling us they needed us separated by male and female first. Within those groupings they would work through the roster by department and rank. One team would take care of the women, and another would take care of the men. She asked that we organize ourselves, forming a line in those groups as they called our names. She said we would start with biodata collection and ID creation. When we each completed that process, we would be directed to an exam room where they would get vitals and draw blood and other specimens for a full workup. Then we would go to radiology for a series of scans.

*That's quite a lot.*

AT: Yes, and if the grumbling that increased to a dull roar was any indication, everyone else thought so as well. But Major Statham handled herself well, climbing on a chair to command attention and refocus the group. She acknowledged that it likely felt very intrusive, but explained that given the fact that we had been through something no one else had ever experienced, they needed to make sure the passage through time and space in such an anomalous way didn't . . . how did she put it? . . . "alter" our "physical bodies." She said there was no way of anticipating what that kind of space travel might do or how being in a no-man's-land for forty years could have impacted us.

*Do you think that's valid? From the perspective of a medical doctor?*

AT: It is hard to say. I think certainly we could have experienced unusual changes. We already knew that astronauts could suffer multiple health problems from prolonged exposure to zero gravity, one of the most significant being loss of bone and muscle mass, and there have been indications of decreased cardiovascular function. We were in a simulated-gravity environment, and, as that was a fairly new technology when we employed it, we did not have any reliable studies of the long-term effects. We definitely have no data on what traveling through a wormhole and being suspended in time could have done. So, yes, I suppose there was some validity to it. That said, I was suspicious of their methods and motives.

*Which seems to have been a good instinct.*

AT: Yes, well, we would come to that conclusion quickly. At that moment, though, our concerns were more immediate. Before we got any further, Michael Li said what we all were thinking, that we'd been away for way longer than we ever imagined possible, and he said he really would like to find out if his brother . . . was . . . what happened to him. He is a very even-keeled fellow, so I knew if the strain was making him this vocal, we definitely were at critical mass. I felt it incumbent upon me to neutralize things, so I asked the major if I could address the team. She gladly gave me the floor. I said, "We have been through too much to come apart at the seams now. If we can just get through this part, we can make a list of the information we need on whom and present it to Major Statham to gather in a way that ensures we all are brought up to speed in an efficient and thorough manner." They all nodded at me, suggesting they were agreeable, though I was not certain how long that would hold.

*How long did it take for these initial tests? There were twenty-six of you, right? That would have taken some time.*

AT: Yes, it did, but we tried to keep everyone going with the flow rather than trying to swim against it. So Major Statham began the roll call with Captain Halverson, who stepped forward, leading by example, and that gave me some hope that we were on track. She proceeded through the list of names, one by one, each person taking their place. She had to remind a few it was not necessary to announce themselves, which seemed a bit unnecessarily curt to me, but I suppose the strain was showing on her as well. She had quite a lot of responsibility dropped in her lap without warning.

*Can't say I blame her. So she started with the women?*

AT: Yes, there were eight of them. Including Captain Halverson and Erica Steele from the bridge, we also had Leila Tate in engineering; my wife, Sarah, Nancy Bolton, and Natalie Flemming, in medical. Brooke Connors and Leigh Lawton were from communications.

*Thank you for giving us their names and recognizing them. They seem to have been a little lost in the wake of everything that has happened.*

AT: I know we are now in a world where the gender balance is heavily skewed to the female, so they do not stand out as much, but these women are extraordinary and deserve acknowledgement for all of their contributions, but especially for how they handled the way we were treated upon our return. They moved quickly and stood silently, stoically, as they awaited next steps. I could not begin to imagine what they were thinking about all of this. Were they wondering what their place would be in this world where they were no longer considered minorities, where they were in power, where they could leave behind the oppression and misogyny they experienced as they fought their way onto this crew? And what of their options for their careers, for finding partners and having families? While that was hardly the priority at the time, it had to be on their minds. Were they contemplating the fates of their male counterparts on the team? Knowing each of them quite well, I feel certain they were.

*Those are very valid thoughts, and a very compassionate view.*

AT: Thank you, but I cannot help but have the utmost respect for them. They were an essential part of our team and instrumental to our survival to this point. And I apparently lost myself in those thoughts because Major Statham had to penetrate my reverie with a sharp, admonishing announcement of my name. I had become the bottleneck in the system and was not fully synced up when she moved on quickly to the others. I suppose I was experiencing a bit of a senior moment. Do you need the names of the other men on the crew?

*We covered many of them with Hunter in his interview, but if you would like to give us a quick rundown, it would be good to have them all together.*

AT: Certainly. So let's see. The names called before mine were from the bridge—Hunter Young, Martin Lucas, and Charles Du Plessis. From communications we had Daniel Cohen, Steven Harris, and Pearce Johnson. Kamil Awan, Michael Li, Byron Rice, Scott Jordan, and Javier Romero were in engineering. Oh, also Kenneth Latham in engineering.

And from the galley we had Sean Flemming—he is the twin brother of Natalie, who was on my medical team. Good kids. Sarah and I have become surrogate . . . Oh, I suppose we are too old to be parents to them, but maybe *very* young grandparents anyway. Then there were Jeremy Chisholm, Miguel Perez, and Lenny Jones in the galley as well.

*This is helpful. Thank you. For someone claiming to have senior moments, you had no trouble recalling all of those names and where they worked. That's impressive.*

AT: Oh, well, that is the easy part for me. I am a people person. I value relationships, and in my book no one is insignificant, regardless of their rank. In fact, I know the stories of how each member of the team came to be on the ship, who they left behind, and what their dreams and aspirations were before things went awry. Of course this is part of cultivating a good bedside manner as a doctor, but it may be a case of the chicken or the egg. Did I develop this trait in my career, or was I drawn to the field because of my gift? I imagine a bit of both. At any rate the technicians began taking scans of our fingerprints and retinas first. I looked to my right and caught my wife's gaze. She looked back at me with dismay, but she seemed to be setting aside her objections to make this whole thing go more smoothly. I was grateful for that. Remarkably, we finished right around dinnertime and the meal was notably better than I expected. I did not find we would be fed that well on an ongoing basis, however. My guess was the spread was an attempt to smooth things over with us, or, as Hunter might say, to keep the natives from getting restless.

*They clearly owed you at least that much. How did you finish out your first night back at home . . . if you could call it "home"?*

AT: Hunter started calling them *pods*—the rooms where we slept—because he said we were being treated like *aliens* they intercepted and were studying. It ended up being only one of many "homes" we would have over the next few weeks, but it was comfortable enough. After dinner I had a feeling Hunter was ready to unload on me as he fell back heavily onto his bunk, shoved his pillow under his head to prop himself up, and sighed heavily. I wanted to make sure we would not be overheard before he got rolling, so I put my hand up, cautioning him to hold his thoughts for the moment. The bays were more glass enclosures than rooms, similar to an ICU room in a hospital. There were curtains to close for privacy, but that did not do much to diminish the fishbowl feel. I closed the door and pulled the curtain, and then sat at the foot of his bed. I leaned back against the wall, let out my own heavy sigh, and opened up the conversation, confessing, "I do not mind saying, I was more than a bit thrown off by the request for certain specimens. It is not exactly routine." Hunter agreed that he did not recall even having to do that when they did our physicals before the expedition launch.

*What do you mean when you say "certain specimens"?*

AT: They asked for sperm samples. There was no justifiable reason for that, so I am not sure why they wanted it. It felt extremely intrusive. I could not fathom what on earth they could possibly learn from that material, which could not be revealed from a blood panel and standard scans. Since I was a physician and scientist, my imagination was going places I found very uncomfortable. I began to think Hunter's paranoia was contagious. Hunter threw fuel on that fire when he reminded me of what they had shared about the population dropping to less than 6 billion in the first years of the pandemic, and that the male portion of the population was most heavily impacted.

*Why did that add to your paranoia?*

AT: Because he revealed to me that while we were going through all of the tests, he managed to find out that the current population was only 2.7 billion! I thought there was no way that could be true. He had to have the number wrong. Then he sat up and leaned in to whisper and looked furtively around the room, as if he suspected there were spies in every corner. He said he asked again to clarify, at which point they got really tight-lipped. Who wouldn't begin to have their own misgivings with all of that? I am not sure the gravity of that information fully sank in for a bit, but it hit me like a ball-peen hammer to the sternum.

*It is fair to say it took the entire world a tragically long time for the gravity of the situation to sink in. The response time was dulled by widespread denial.*

AT: This was far more dire than I had thought. I could not even begin to process the ramifications of such an event, such a shift in culture. As much as I wanted to get out of there to check on friends and family, I was just as eager to find out how much the world had changed. Hunter commented on the notable difference of women running the show. I was inclined to think that was probably a good thing. We men were sure making a mess of it all. He said he saw a few glitches in that theory. I was a bit disappointed in what I thought he was suggesting. He said he had meant nothing so misogynistic as hormone issues, just that, as the saying goes, "Power corrupts; absolute power corrupts absolutely," and people are just people. He pointed out that being in control does strange things to people in ways you would not expect. And I agreed. Those were wise and thoughtful observations. Of course he did show his true colors a bit when he added, "And we all know women can be ruthless when they need to be . . . and in far more cunning ways than men. We tend to use brute force to get our way. They are more crafty." I told my friend it seemed he had some trust issues. He said he had just been on the receiving end of some of that fury that hell cannot even match. I suggested we put a pin in that for the time being and move on to the fact that he was right about the flow of information slowing to a trickle.

We needed to figure out a way to pull more out of them because they would not be forthcoming on their own. Hunter was leaning toward a shock-and-awe approach. That didn't sound like the measured . . . or sane . . . approach I had in mind. He explained we should make a list of all the questions we wanted answered and just hit Statham with them rapid-fire in the morning . . . in front of everyone, put her on the spot so she could not evade or avoid us any longer. I wasn't sure that was the best idea. I felt we would do well to cultivate some goodwill with her. At the moment they just seemed like they were our captors. If we gave them reason to panic, we might actually be locked down. Of course

Hunter said we already were. I was not ready to make that leap, but I still thought we were going to get more of what we wanted if we used a less aggressive approach.

He started to raise further objections, and I knew we could end up having to resort to his methods at some point, but to start, I felt we needed them *wanting* to work with us. Still, I conceded some ground and said, "I do agree that making a list of questions we need answered is helpful. How about we start working on that tonight? Maybe we can assign some to others on our team who can collect info as well." He agreed to do it "my" way, but insisted that if we didn't get some satisfactory answers within twenty-four hours, he was coming out with both guns blazing.

*That was not an idle threat, was it?*

AT: No, indeed, it was not. The next day he did behave himself . . . for the most part.

*Thank you, Dr. Tilden. We can take a break now. I'd like to bring in your wife when we resume.*

AT: Thank you for speaking with me. I am at your disposal, unless someone decides I should not be.

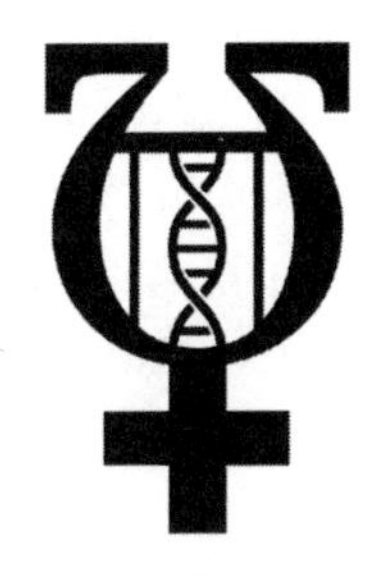

# CHAPTER FIVE

## A SHADOW OF OUR FORMER SELVES

*Mrs. Tilden, thank you for joining us.*

Sarah Tilden (ST): Please call me Sarah.

*Okay. Sarah, I have talked with Abe about your first day in the medical facility. Is there anything you'd like to add from your perspective?*

ST: I am confident my husband gave you more than enough detail on that. Just tell me where he left off and I'll pick up there.

*He covered your first day at Miramar. We were just about to get into Hunter's behavior on the second day.*

ST: I see. Well, we reassembled in the morning. I noted Abe must have given Hunter a good talking-to because he was so gracious to Lydia. In fact, he was so courteous to her that it seemed to throw her off her game a bit. That said, it looked like his civility train might come off the rails as soon as it started down the tracks when he said he was hoping for more disclosure. Thankfully, he just had a wobbly start. He apologized, explaining he did not mean to be antagonistic. It was just that he felt they were subjecting us to a death by a thousand cuts and we'd be better off if they just gave it all to us straight in one dose.

*Having talked with him, I agree that does seem uncharacteristically restrained.*

ST: It was. However, he was hardly the one we had to worry about that day. Dr. Awan was worked into quite a lather that morning. Desperate to get a report on his family, he pressed Lydia for information. She promised she would do her best to get some details for everyone soon, but she advised him he had to be prepared for the fact that his wife . . . his children . . . would also need time to process this information, and may not know how to accept him back into their lives. Can you just imagine? That poor man. At that point she turned to all of us and said this would be true across the board with spouses, partners, children, parents. She said the only thing she could tell us right then was that some of us would find our loved ones were no longer living. Some of us would find they had moved on to build families with other spouses or partners. Reentering their lives at this stage, and considering the age differences now in play, could be very difficult, if not impossible.

My goodness, that put a fine point on it. Her words sent a ripple of harsh truth through everyone. I heard soft sobs and gasps fluttering through the group as they started to take down such a very bitter pill. Even though Abe had asked me to be sensitive to everyone else, I couldn't help but slip my hand in his and give him a little squeeze. We both felt so torn between our deep gratitude for having each other and the grief we felt for our team and their loss. I had no intention of flaunting our fortune, but I needed his touch for reassurance, if just briefly. Then I carefully released his hand and, in an attempt to shift the attention to another topic, I asked, "Major, can you just give us a summary of the major changes in the main areas of interest?"

*What kinds of things were you interested in knowing? Abe said he and Hunter were making a list. Did they have that ready?*

ST: Yes, they did. Abe started the ball rolling by asking for some sense of what was going on politically around the world—what had changed in the government, in science. I interjected with my own curiosity about religion and the arts. Martin wanted to know about sports, pointing out that most of it was played by men, and mostly watched by men too. He definitely hit on something there. There really was a lot of our culture that catered to male interests, and even I wondered how it had been affected. Before anyone else could chime in, Major Statham asked everyone to slow down and not to ask everything at once. She said she would have preferred to do this in the conference room, but it was pretty obvious she wasn't going to get anything else out of us until we got some answers, so she asked us to take a seat. We began pulling together chairs and benches, which were scattered around the lab.

*It must have been overwhelming for her to figure out where to start.*

ST: I would have thought so. I certainly would have been a scattered mess, but she dove right in with what we learned the day before about the pandemic reducing the global population to 2.7 billion—just unfathomable. She explained that, of those people, 15 percent, or approximately 400 million, are male. None are under the age of thirty, most between the ages of forty and sixty-five. But that number continues to decline. That still seemed like a lot of men to me, so I asked why so much had changed in the social construct. She said that fifteen men for every one hundred women, when the male/female ratio used to be about half and half, is far more significant than it sounds. That did put things into perspective. It had most obviously affected the male-dominated areas of our society—the military and governing organizations, in particular—and while there are some men in leadership roles, such as General Dunne, the heads of state are primarily women. Also, the military is comprised *entirely* of women. There are men of the age to serve, but she said they are considered a protected class today, in case a cure is found. No one wants to risk any harm coming to the men.

*The numbers are hard to comprehend. It really takes seeing the impact firsthand to drive it home.*

ST: I'm sure that is true. Her explanation seemed to create a bit of intrigue though—especially among the younger men of our crew who begin laughing and nudging each other. I'm sure it won't come as a surprise to you that their imaginations were running wild. All they saw were the perks this new dynamic could involve. Hunter, in his unique way, put them in their place. I would never use words like this, but for the sake of giving you an accurate depiction of who he was, I will quote him. He said, "Hey, jinglenuts, calm yourselves. You all could be the last men on Earth and still wouldn't score, so let the major finish."

*Well, I definitely can imagine him saying that, but hearing you say it, feels a little uncomfortable, I'll admit.*

ST: You are blushing as much as Lydia did. It seems the bawdy locker-room talk that was standard in the military was no longer tolerated, which makes perfect sense given the fact that little of that was tolerated in society after the "Me Too Movement" that arose in the years before our mission. Lydia tried to get us back on course, diving back into her presentation by sharing that due to the declining population, many economies and states collapsed. President Marshall touched on that when she met with us the day before, but Lydia explained a bit more, telling us that a special World Council was convened to make decisions on a global scale, and they voted to aggregate resources, leadership, and governments into regions. She said the areas that were the least impacted *naturally* became the capitals for these new regions, as they had the best means for controlling the impact.

*Yes, that's why President Marshall was introduced as President of the Americas. Hunter told us he picked up on it and asked. He really is very attuned.*

ST: Yes, he definitely has a nose for that sort of thing. And it may have taken a full day of repeatedly asking, but he finally got his answer. She clarified that we are no longer just the United States of America. I had heard of these regional designations that global organizations had been using for decades to study population growth and decline, as well as climate shifts and other information that impacts the planet. I think it was pretty smart for them to simply use those to create the new zones. From what I understand, President Marshall is the president of the Americas, which includes North America, Latin America, and the Caribbean—she said the fifty states of the US still exist, but the lines are starting to get blurred, which I find a bit troubling. Seems like a disaster just waiting to happen. But you've seen enough of that lately, so maybe it wouldn't be so bad. Anyway, I digress. Lydia said the other regions are Africa, Asia, Western Europe, Eastern Europe, and Oceania. Though I am not able to really conceptualize how the Oceania region would work, since it is just a bunch of unconnected islands.

*They operate with a less structured governing body than the other regions. They are so spread out geographically that the region operates pretty much independently. Their populations are very isolated and don't number more than about 4 million total.*

ST: Okay. I suppose they have figured out how to make that work. We learned that the capital of Africa is located in what once was South Africa, which makes sense. It has been one of the most developed and commercially progressive areas on the continent—not so much the Third World we think of when Africa comes to mind. China is still a significant power, even though they were really weakened by the plague, and they are the center of the Asian region. That does not surprise me. I honestly expected China to take over the Western World within the decade . . . well, the decade we were in when we left.

What did surprise me a bit was that I expected Western Europe to be controlled by England, but they didn't endure the impact of the epidemic well. Germany is now the hub of governing. I have to confess that does send a bit of a chill up my spine, as someone whose parents were children of the Holocaust. But that is another time and another regime, I assume. Hopefully, democracy held there. Of course, it in no way shocked me to learn Eastern Europe is still dominated by Russia. Lydia said they are in a very vulnerable state and are barely surviving, but that is also nothing new. The one thing I can't seem to get my head around is how they managed to get all of these individual countries to merge. That seems like a lot to coordinate, even with the groupings somewhat built in.

*It was a combination of a new type of leadership—women—and the recognition that this was the only way for the human race to survive. There really weren't any power plays because the aggregation just sort of happened organically.*

ST: I can see that. Lydia told us the war over possession of the corn and the technology to propagate it rendered a lot of territory uninhabitable—so tragic. She said there was such desperation to gain the upper hand that some governments made targeted strikes of dirty bombs on the fields of corn we were growing in different areas of the world. Talk about drinking poison in the hope of harming your enemy! That, of course, led to retaliation on regions where stolen corn was being cultivated . . . The things we do to each other because of greed and fear . . . it really breaks my heart. And those who have the greatest vulnerabilities are always the ones to suffer the most, like the countries hit hardest by famine and economic crises. They were just about decimated because they used the corn the longest. Then they had insult added to injury by having their land destroyed.

*That seems to be the way of the world—many suffer for the whims of a few.*

ST: Well, it was the way of the world run by men. I had hoped for better with women at the helm. I guess we all are human and subject to human weakness.

*The people who were left in those countries began migrating to more populated areas and all of the immigration concerns that had been so prominent were basically moot. Things have begun to right themselves environmentally, but most regions were left with such limited resources, the people who used to be spread out across our country and the rest of the world have stayed mostly aggregated in population centers.*

ST: I suppose it was wise to band together to keep various institutions running, meeting the basic needs of life, and holding things together in case you found a way out of the mess.

*Exactly. The EU that already had a common currency and other conglomerated structures just became the Western European Union, though some of the Slavic states split off to become part of the Eastern European Union. That model was employed in the other regions, though all of this has been leading us toward a global government and a global currency. We were on the brink of making that move. Who knows how that might change given your return?*

ST: I just can't bring myself to think about how we might figure into that.

*Then let's not, for now. Why don't we move on to the rest of what you learned about the New World Order?*

ST: Yes, well, I'm sure we got the *Reader's Digest* version of it all . . . Oh, do you know what that is? Am I using an outdated reference there?

*I am familiar with the phrase.*

ST: Okay. Well, if she had tried to fill in every detail, it would be enough to fill a whole college semester, I think. But the highlights were these: She started by reassuring us that what we knew as the United States is mostly still in tact, though we had acquired portions of Mexico along the border prior to the pandemic, as well as Cuba. Although, if I remember correctly, that was in the works when we left. It just wrecked me to hear that some of the states had become virtual wastelands in the process of eradicating the crops of corn. I assume she means the Plains States—Middle America. What she described about the regions we now have sounds much like the "Red and Blue States" we had, so I guess they still exist, but are clustered mostly on each coast. I'll say that division is one thing I'd hoped we wouldn't return to, but it sounds like they aren't quite as polarized as they once were, perhaps mostly out of necessity.

*Yes, that's true, though that doesn't stop people from disagreeing just as ferociously when there is a reason. I suspect that fracture will widen now, after the news of your return.*

ST: I suppose some things never truly change. Unfortunately for those like our young men, the same doesn't hold true for sporting events. Lydia said you do still manage to provide some diversions and entertainment, but organizations such as the NFL, NBA, and MLB are gone, and those initials . . . they are about the extent of my professional sports knowledge! I'm not really a fan, though that probably comes as no surprise. But none of the global regions participate in competitive sports any longer, nor do we have the Olympics. Even though I don't have a favorite sports team, I still cannot fathom a world like that. I did not enjoy watching it, and neither did Abe, but I know it was part of our culture, and an important part of our economy.

*Yeah, it just wasn't financially sustainable. Sports, the opera and theater, movies, books—all of those things were considered luxuries that fell to the side when everyone was in survival mode.*

ST: Such a travesty. You know, humans need artistic and creative expression to survive. It's part of how we are made. I just can't imagine books being considered a luxury. They are a necessity. They are how information is shared. I am guessing that's especially true if the internet has been affected by all of this. We became really accustomed to having everything you want to know at the touch of a button. But if that is no longer as viable and available as it was in our time, I don't know how you have adjusted.

*It's true, and people do still seek out those diversions. It's just not a profit-making industry anymore. Even religion, which had become big business, with megachurches and famous TV preachers, has gone back to a far simpler way of functioning.*

ST: There is a lot about this that is disappointing, but I can see where there would be a lot of benefit for our society.

*And just to set your mind at ease, books still exist, though the electronic libraries are limited. The war compromised a lot of the infrastructure for communication—the internet, broad mobile-phone coverage—and those are only available in the most populated areas. The cost of rebuilding the cell towers that were destroyed in the war has been nearly prohibitive. Security also became an issue and everyone was afraid to use those devices, so I guess you could say we are back to a more analog way of living.*

ST: Well, I'll tell you, many of the younger set on our crew don't know of a time before you could carry your phone and a world of information in your pocket. I was born in 1969, which seems impossible as I sit in 2065, still living and breathing and feeling quite young. But I saw this technology develop and change the world I knew.

*That is remarkable. And how old are you, Abe?*

AT: I am . . . or was fifty-eight when we left.

*How strange to imagine that at relatively young ages, the two of you are most likely the oldest people on the planet.*

AT: Imagine that! I had not considered it, but, if you take into account the forty years we lost, that probably is technically true.

*Well, let me be the first to tell you, you both look spectacular for your age! Is there anything else we've left out?*

ST: Let's see . . . oh, we all had a particular interest in the area of science. So, even though we were already getting quite exhausted from the information download, we perked up when Lydia started down this road. She told us that all funding for innovation or research and development to expand scientific knowledge was diverted from any area that didn't directly relate to finding a cure for the virus, including no further space exploration. This was especially hard for us to hear. I think even our young men were more let down by this than the loss of their favorite football team. There is no more going to the depths of the sea to study sea life. Technological advancements are at a virtual standstill. Just devastating news.

*Again, it's a shift in priorities to what is needed for survival. The determining factor is where we should invest our limited resources of funds, mental energies, time, and manpower.*

ST: Interesting that you call it *manpower*. I guess that sort of vernacular is still kind of embedded.

*I guess it would sound strange to you, but, in some ways, it does refer to men specifically. We don't have many, and their unique physiology is needed for certain tasks. We have to be very judicious about how we use that particular resource, since we don't have a way of making more at this point.*

ST: Don't let Hunter hear you call him a resource. He would be fit to be tied over that!

*Oh, it's not like that. We are considered a cherished species. Endangered even.*

ST: Well, I'm not sure his ego needs to hear that either! Of course the young men on the crew found the gender ratios to be very encouraging. I overheard Hunter giving the boys a hard time about it. Something like: "Lucas, you and Harris can stop congratulating yourselves." Martin gave it right back to him, saying, "We can't do any worse than you, Commander." Of course Hunter pulled rank. "Easy. I'm still your superior . . . in every way, I might add. And you know I'm just busting your chops." That isn't the word he used, but that's all I will say. Then he told them they'd better be careful what they wish for. They just might get it. Doesn't that seem to be a recurring theme? These young men have no clue what they'd be signing up for.

*They just might find out.*

ST: I have a feeling you are right about that. That was where the information session ended for the time being. Lydia said they needed to get on with the testing. Everyone on our team let her know quickly they were not happy about being treated like lab mice. And she let us know just as quickly that our opinion wasn't exactly a consideration. She told us we were going to be subjected to this for the next two to three days, and then it would be over. She asked us to consider how much easier it would be if we just accepted this fact and allowed it to happen. And with that, we were shuttled off to different compartments of the lab to be poked and prodded.

*Sarah, I've enjoyed speaking with you. And, Abe, thanks for sticking around. I think we are good for now. I'll be in touch if I need follow-up.*

# CHAPTER SIX
## MAKING WAVES

**0200 HOURS, MEDICAL POD**
**COME ALONE**

*[Note to reader: This interview was conducted shortly after the incident reported and, in large part, was the impetus for this documentary. Major Lydia Statham has been unavailable for follow-up questions since. The note above was sent in an unmarked envelope, along with a phone number, which I used to contact her, but discovered was deactivated immediately after our conversation.]*

*Major . . . this is Major Statham, correct?*

*[silence]*

*Hello?*

LS: Yes.

*You asked me to call you. What is this about?*

LS: There are things you need to know . . . about the *Alpha Centauri* crew.

*Is something wrong with them?*

LS: Something is very wrong. But . . . not with them . . . with what's happening to them.

*Go ahead.*

*[silence]*

*Major, you can take whatever time you need; it's your dime. But I kind of need to know where this is headed.*

LS: It's about the last night they were at Miramar . . . the last time I saw them.

*Okay. You have my attention.*

LS: You got the note I sent.

*Yes. What is it?*

LS: I sent it to Hunter . . . Commander Young . . . asking him to meet with me. I thought he would be the right person to talk to. When he showed up, he shoved the note in my face, demanding an explanation. I knew I was taking a really big risk, especially given the inflammatory nature of his personality, but I couldn't, in good conscience, let this lie. He seemed, to me, to be the most capable of doing something smart with the information.

*What couldn't you let lie?*

LS: I'm getting to that. He was just as impatient, and really noisy to boot. I shushed him and asked him not to alert the entire compound. I said I really thought he'd be better at this. I picked him because I thought he had a grasp of the art of subterfuge. I was beginning to question my judgment and turned to walk away, but really only to make a point.

I wasn't actually planning on leaving; I'd taken too much of a risk not to follow through, and he knew it, but played along and stopped me before I could take more than a step. He asked me to wait and give him a minute to catch up. He said he'd really had it with all of the cagey bullshit they'd been enduring and just wanted me to cut to the chase.

*So, what were you going to tell him?*

LS: I couldn't do it out there in the open. I had to suss him out first, to see if I had read him right. I told him, a little louder than expected, that he needed to go back to his quarters. Before he could go off on me—and, believe me, he was revving up for it—I grabbed his hand and pressed a piece of paper into it. He just looked at me with an expression of mingled confusion and exasperation. I whispered to him, "Turn around and head back toward your room. When you get to the corridor, use the grid on this paper to guide you back to the utility closet beyond the medical hub. Follow the steps I've mapped out exactly. It will take you there by way of the blind spots. I'll be waiting for you." He started objecting, muttering about blind spots, complaining about being made to jump through a bunch of hoops like a trained monkey, thinking it was another test of some sort.

*It's becoming clear why he might have felt that way. You've yet to offer any useful information.*

LS: As I told him, there is something I need to tell you, but nearly every inch of that place was under surveillance. We couldn't speak openly about what he needed to know. And I'm probably under surveillance now.

*Wait. What? Why?*

LS: Don't worry about that now. I told him ten minutes. If he wasn't there by then, I'd be gone. Then in full voice again, I said, "Thank you for your cooperation, Commander. I understand you are restless, but we need you to stay in your quarters after hours. Good night. I hope you can get some sleep. We have a long day tomorrow." I had to justify for anyone watching why we would have been out in the hallways. It didn't look like anyone had seen us, and I felt safe to head in the opposite direction. I prayed some sense would prevail over him and he would follow my instructions. I waited in the closet for him to arrive. It was cramped and dark, but safe from prying eyes and ears. I have to say, when the door creaked open and a sliver of light pierced the void where I stowed myself, I had the faintest imagining, the quickest flash of a notion of what the crew might have experienced when they bounced out of wherever they were hiding all those years . . . decades. I was just about to abort the mission when Young slipped in without the subtlety I'd hoped for. I scolded him in hushed but harsh words. To be honest, I think he could do with a little more chastisement in his life.

*You'll get no argument here. But, what did you have to tell him?*

LS: I'm getting to that. I asked him why he was late. I was about ready to leave. I had to know if it was because he was detained by someone in the compound. If so, the meeting was off. He said Abe woke up and found him gone and went looking for him. They ran into each other in the corridor and Hunter had to convince him to go back to the room. That freaked me out, I must admit. I was afraid he had aroused too much suspicion. He assured me he hadn't. He said, "Contrary to your pervading opinion, I am not an idiot. While Abe is trustworthy, I don't know what I'm getting into at the moment, and I'm not about to drag him into it too." I wasn't all that comforted by this; however, in for a penny, in for a pound, I guess, so I went ahead.

*Great. What did you tell him?*

LS: I said I was sure he had noticed the information was flowing very slowly. He called it a *trickle*. Fair point. So I explained that part of it was legitimately because there was so much to disseminate and we were trying not to overwhelm them. That much was genuine.

*Understood, but not exactly a big revelation. Get to the good stuff.*

LS: Okay, okay. You know, I'm taking as much of a risk as you are, so ease up a little.

*This is for your benefit. You are probably running out of time. Why risk all of this and not get to the point?*

LS: *Fine.* I told him there was another part of this that was difficult because we really didn't know how to deal with them. We were in completely uncharted territory on so many levels. We didn't have a clue about all the ways their return was going to impact the world. He got a bit annoyed at this point, asking if I had summoned him to a coat closet in the middle of the night, and had him run an obstacle course to boot, only to tell him what he already knew, complaining that he could have stayed in bed and had the same information he had so far.

*The feeling is mutual. I don't know what time it is where you are, but here it's after 2 a.m.*

LS: Trust me, this is necessary, and relevant. He said they were beginning to feel gaslighted, or led on, or whatever the term was for this ridiculously protracted exercise in futility. And he wasn't wrong. I got it. He didn't trust me or anyone else, but I asked him to bear with me as I attempted to figure out how to communicate some gut feelings that were hard to quantify.

*Gut feelings?*

LS: Hunter questioned it too, but, as I said to him, don't pretend like you don't let your own gut feelings guide you. You wouldn't have responded to my note if you didn't sense something was . . . askew. I'm just asking you to trust mine too.

*Fine. But enough with the suspense, okay? I'm as much of a sucker for the clandestine as the next guy, but everyone has their limits.*

LS: Well, just as I told Hunter, I don't know a lot, which was the first thing that had me worried. I just know that the crew had seriously thrown everyone for a loop, and I didn't just mean they didn't know where to put everyone; I meant that they—the Powers that Be—were losing their shit. Lots of closed-door conversations with the highest-ranking officials: incessant, heated whispering and an air of heavy anxiety everywhere. Hunter might have been frustrated with the lack of information, but I'm telling you, I was not getting much more from the higher-ups.

*What does that mean?*

LS: I'm not really sure. Hunter didn't like that answer much and he started to leave. I grabbed his arm before he could open the door and pulled him back. I knew if I let him go, I wouldn't get him back, and while I didn't have much to offer, he needed to hear what I had to say. I told him I was sorry I didn't have the kind of answers he was looking for . . . really, just more questions, but the fact that I had questions should have been an answer for him on some level. I hadn't been read in and I was supposed to be running at least part of the show. That shouted volumes to me, and it should have to him too. I told him something shady was going on, and I did not get the sense they were going to let any of the crew go after they finished running the tests. My guess is that they were under lock and key for more than their safety. Honestly, I didn't think . . . still don't . . . that they plan on releasing them to the wild . . . ever.

*What makes you say that?*

LS: The fact that they were being transferred, for one. And that it was happening under serious cover, for another. We haven't used a special ops team in years. I'm not even sure how they pulled one together.

*Where are they taking them?*

LS: As I said, it was happening in secret. I didn't know and I have . . . or had . . . a pretty high level of security clearance.

*When is it happening?*

LS: You're not listening to me. It's done . . . or will be by morning. Look, all I can tell you . . . all I know to tell you . . . is that they were acting like the crew is manna from heaven and a blight on the world simultaneously. I've never seen them in such a tailspin, and it makes me really uneasy about where all of this is leading. I anticipate a time coming in the not-too-distant future when they will be confronted with forming some alliances and making some hard choices, and I have a feeling they may not find themselves wanting to come down on the side of this country they served so faithfully. In fact, this country may prove to be an even greater enemy than those they always thought they had to fight.

*Commander Young strikes me as having a fairly healthy skepticism of the government. Did he heed your warnings?*

LS: That's part of why I chose him to talk to about this. He was a bit surprised when I said his dossier helped me decide whom to approach, which I found odd. He said it's just different when it goes from speculation, which most people call *paranoid delusion*, to being confirmed by a reliable source. He seemed like he was gearing up for a rant, but I needed to finish before we got busted. I had already pushed the envelope about as far as I could, so I cut him off. I told him the bottom line was that I felt I owed it to them to make sure someone was really on top of things. I have no idea what my role will be, once they are taken to a new location, or how much access I will have to information I could share with them. I'm not certain I will even have access to any of them anymore.

*Well, I'm not really sure what to do with this wealth of information you've given me.*

LS: Yeah, yeah. I know it sounds very cryptic, but that's all I've got. Just as I told Hunter, keep your wits about you and don't take anything at face value.

*I never do, Major. I never do.*

LS: Hunter slipped out the door at that point. At least he was more cautious going out than he was coming in. I waited a moment before taking leave of our rendezvous point myself. As I rounded the corner to make my way back to my own quarters, I came up short, finding myself face-to-face with glaring, accusatory eyes. She said, "I know what you're doing."

*Oh, hell. You were caught?*

LS: I was sure I was, but I just tried to ask as innocently as possible, "What are you talking about?" She repeated, "I know what you are doing, and you're not going to get away with it." I got a little indignant with her, trying to cover, snapping, "Spears, I really don't know what you mean, but I suggest you watch your tone. I am your superior officer." That's when she said the strangest thing to me. She said, "You can't jump the line . . . *ma'am*." Now I was not only lost, I was really annoyed by the snarky way she threw in the *ma'am*. I thought she was onto my sharing confidential information. Apparently, she thought there was something else going on, but it's beyond me what that is. I was just so relieved she didn't really know what I was doing that I let the other go, but I told her she should not be roaming the halls past curfew and ordered her back to her quarters. She said she was on night watch, so I told her to get back to her post or I'd have to report her. She turned on her heels and disappeared around the corner.

I never like to pull rank, but sometimes I'm glad I have it to pull, but I'm sure it's only going to cover me so far. I can't risk word getting up the chain that I was breaking protocol or, worse, violating direct orders. I don't really have any leverage over her other than rank, and I'm not sure that's enough anymore to keep people in line. Blind submission to authority is something that went out with the patriarchy. The only loyalty we have now comes from what's necessary for survival. Maybe that will be enough. Regardless, I needed time to get my head around what's happening and was trying to get some better information to Young. I don't like what my gut says is coming. I haven't gamed out all of the possibilities; my head is just swimming with fragments of crazy scenarios. All I know is something just feels . . . off . . . and I have a nagging fear that this is going to get really messy. That's why I reached out to you.

*I will do some digging and see what I can find on my end. Can I use this number to contact you again?*

LS: I don't . . . I'll have to . . . Shit, I have to go . . .

*[At this point the line went dead. When I tried to reach her again, it was disconnected. I will continue attempting to reestablish contact with her, but I'm not hopeful.]*

# CHAPTER SEVEN
## AN INCONVENIENT TRUTH

*Sir, would you please state your name and rank for the record?*

SD: General Stephen K. Dunne.

*Thank you, sir. I understand you are taking a big risk and defying direct orders by speaking with me today. I appreciate your willingness for disclosure.*

SD: There was nothing about this that went down well. Not a damn thing. I knew there was no way we could continue to hold those people and keep them a secret for as long as the administration wanted. Honestly, I didn't know how we kept it under wraps as long as we did. I'm a company man. I serve at the pleasure of the president. What they were proposing . . . it was just unconscionable! I was powerless to change the trajectory, but I can't in good conscience let it go down in history the way it is being spun.

*General, that is my goal as well. What can you tell me about the first cabinet meeting to discuss plans for the crew?*

SD: Well, I sat looking around this big expensive mahogany table—the kind that would suggest important, smart, experienced people meet here—and saw the dumbstruck expression on every face, which confirmed for me that we were flying by the seat of our pants. It was not a comforting scene. It was an all-too-familiar sight, and one would think we'd be prepared for dealing with inconceivable scenarios by now. But *this* was one for the books.

*So no one had a handle on the situation?*

SD: Not even close. President Marshall had asked me to work with the intelligence director to assess our exposure. I anticipated this, as it was obviously under my purview as Chairman of the Joint Chiefs, so I already had them working on it. But I informed the president that the spirit of cooperation we'd had with the other governments was going to be seriously compromised if they got wind of us trying to find out if they knew we'd done something they would surely see as underhanded. It was a lot harder to go out and ask about chatter when there really hadn't been anything to chatter about of late. Not without raising suspicions.

*That must have been tricky.*

SD: It was, and I don't think President Marshall really got it because she asked us to see what we could find out anyway. She didn't want to keep flying blind on this, which I understood, of course, but our exposure was not limited to pissing off a foreign government, and I don't think that was registering.

*What do you mean?*

SD: Legal exposure. Attorney General Miranda Ford was in the room, and I was looking to her to see if she could keep us on track and steer us out of the murky waters I saw presenting themselves here. President Marshall didn't seem to be seeing beyond the moment of crisis management. She did acknowledge we were in very delicate territory from a human rights perspective.

*It certainly seems to be shaping up that way.*

SD: President Marshall indicated she thought we could justify detaining them for a bit longer for national and personal security reasons, but that didn't give us enough time to get at the primary purpose for containing them and the news of their arrival. This was an incredibly tricky situation, and no one else in that room appeared to have any clue of the Pandora's box we were sitting on. They only thought they knew what was coming. And President Marshall was still dancing around it with the cabinet, which was not a smart play.

*What was she dancing around?*

SD: I really have to spell this out for you? I guess if the surgeon general wasn't getting it, I shouldn't expect you to. Susan Andrews is a bright woman, but not really quick-witted. President Marshall lit into her about not being ahead of the curve on this and considering the potential. Although, to be fair, we had not shared much information with them so far. Just as with the crew, we were dipping our toe into the pool to see how they would respond to the information and the implications.

*What exactly was she missing?*

SD: President Marshall was convinced they could have the cure. SG Andrews began firing questions at her about the findings of their testing and when she could get her hands on that data. Apparently, she hadn't read her brief on the meeting. Typical. I know the brief was . . . *brief* . . . but we weren't sending this stuff out to kill more trees. It wasn't any better in my day, but things are different now. Everything matters, and showing up unprepared was inexcusable.

*What was in the briefing memo?*

SD: It included what we knew so far, which was that their Y-chromosome mapping was still active. It might not be a cure, but we . . . She was hopeful about exploring the possibility of using them to repopulate the planet.

*I'm not sure I understand . . . Surely, she didn't mean . . .*

SD: Oh, she most certainly did. I understand the danger we are facing as a species, but this . . . forcing them into a stud farm? I just was not sure we could make a moral case for that . . . or a legal one, for that matter. And then there was the fight we would have on our hands with the other global powers. They would not only feel entitled to unfettered access—as they should—they were likely to feel an even greater need for this "resource" because they were hit harder. Not to mention the crew members who weren't US citizens.

*I'm not sure I'm tracking with you. How was she proposing we do that?*

SD: She explained we would collect their "genetic material" and begin distributing it to any uninfected women remaining in the population and then to those who have been vaccinated and are likely to sustain a viable pregnancy. AG Ford was about to raise all sorts of objections. I could see it on her face before she opened her mouth. So could the president, and she stopped her, saying she knew this was *unpalatable*, but it could be our only hope. "Unpalatable"? "Unpalatable"?!

*That's one word for it, for sure.*

SD: Miranda still got her concerns voiced. She pointed out that there were some serious issues here—not just the legal issues around detaining them. I was surprised at the language she used and her candor when she called it "really sketchy shit." But she was right. It is. We were talking about forcing them to give up their sperm so we could artificially inseminate women we deemed *acceptable*! Who did we think we were? I guess I should have been thankful we weren't actually going to pimp them out . . . At least, that wasn't on the table yet, but I wasn't sure it wouldn't be. Again, part of why I am talking to you.

*Well, we have missed the boat on doing anything to stop it, but the public still should know.*

SD: AG Ford reminded her that even if we could somehow define this as service to the country and compel them under a national emergency, not all of the crew are . . . or were . . . US citizens. We don't have jurisdiction over all of them. Which then brought up the issue of holding foreign nationals. President Marshall told her this is why she was in the meeting, but she needed all of us to think outside the box. She was convinced this could be our singular chance for reversing the devastation we had endured and were continuing to face. She said even though our greatest minds had been working for thirty years to find a way to reverse this, they were no closer to finding a solution. She asked how could we not consider the possibilities of what she referred to as "a miracle that quite literally landed on our doorstep."

*I understand thinking outside the box, but this seems out in left field.*

SD: Susan got into that. She said that aside from the legal considerations, and even the scientific ones, she wasn't sure we were *supposed* to reverse this—that maybe we were playing God. She went on to say that not just from a moral perspective, but from a scientific mind-set as well, one could argue that this pandemic was a thinning of the herd. It was natural selection doing its thing, as it does from time to time, and it was something we needed to let happen. Her point was that we've been meddling in Mother Nature's business for far too long, and maybe this pandemic was her way of pushing back.

*That is pretty heady and probably wouldn't go over well from a PR standpoint. What is your take on it?*

SD: I think it's worth considering, but I'm not sure we as humans are really ready to let go of our need to control everything. In fact, I doubt it. At that point I felt it was time for me to speak up, so I said, "Madam President, as a man who has dedicated his life to serving this country . . . and just as a man, period, I can say this much. If I were presented with this problem and told I could be a part of the solution, I would be willing to do my part, whatever that might be. However, if you forced me into it, I would fight you every step of the way. It's not okay to take control of someone else's body. Even if it is for the greater good."

*That sounds reasonable.*

SD: I thought so, but President Marshall's response was that while she appreciated my perspective, and respected it—which is probably the most condescending thing you can say to an advisory—she asked what the hell I thought vaccines are all about. We made the whole world get the vaccine for the virus . . . and they still didn't know about the tracking mechanism that went with it. She reasoned that we have been violating rights for the greater good in one way or another pretty much since the beginning of humanity. It's an ugly, inconvenient truth, but a truth nonetheless.

*Wait, what's this about a* tracking device*?*

*[At this point General Dunne asked for a break, and when he returned with his attorney, we agreed to keep that last statement off the record for a limited amount of time, with the understanding that it would be part of the final documentary disclosed after he retired from the administration.]*

SD: We had a century's worth (or more) of precedent for requiring certain things in the interests of public health, and that's what we were going on. Also, we weren't going to get anywhere with Susan's suggestion that we do nothing. Still, I didn't know if I could support this. If ordered, I would have to comply, but I had to come up with a way to convince her otherwise. This just didn't sit well. From the uncomfortable looks on the faces of the other cabinet members, I was not alone. And, to her credit, President Marshall didn't exactly look pleased to be saying any of this. She did seem deeply troubled. She also didn't look like she had slept since this "gift" dropped out of the sky. I knew this wasn't the end of the discussion, and there was time to consider alternatives. I just wasn't sure how many of those we had, but I needed a break, so I excused myself to go over to the Pentagon and check in with my intelligence team. I felt it should be done in person to avoid as much telecommunication as possible. She asked me to report right away if they had any insights or information. I had a feeling I was going to get an earful when I got over there. I just wasn't relishing the report I would have to give her. When I stepped out of the situation room into the hallway, I almost felt like I had the bends. Have you ever experienced that?

*I'm not sure I know what that is.*

SD: I guess not. Deep-sea diving isn't a common form of recreation anymore. It's called decompression sickness—the bends—and it happens when you rise from deep underwater too quickly and your body can't adapt to the change in pressure. It causes pain all over your body and vision disturbances. Anyway, I felt like I had surfaced too fast into a really ugly reality. I leaned against the wall and tried to catch my breath, but my chest was pounding and my head was throbbing. If I hadn't just had a physical of my own, I'd have worried I might be having a heart attack. The young women standing guard by the door didn't know whether they should step in or not. They knew better than to leave their post without permission, but were obviously concerned seeing a superior officer in the state I was in. I waved them off and straightened myself. Not exactly conduct becoming of an officer, but these were unusual circumstances, and there just didn't seem to be an end to them. Thirty years' worth of madness and inconceivable devastation. How much more could we take before humanity just broke completely? Meanwhile, Susan's suggestion kept echoing in my mind. Was it possible we were supposed to let it happen? I just couldn't imagine it, but I also couldn't get it out of my head. But I had more pressing matters to attend to.

*So, what did you find out from your intelligence team?*

SD: Unfortunately, it was exactly what I feared. Two of our embedded agents in the region informed us the Africans knew about the ship. Agent Samantha Roberts was giving me the report. I asked her if she had any notion as to how they got this information, since they were not exactly positioned to have seen it falling out of the sky, and their space program fell apart with the plague. This was not what I wanted to hear, and my head started spinning again. It seemed she could read that on my face because she had the same look of concern as the two guards in the West Wing. But she continued.

She said it seemed they still manned the existing stations, simply monitoring the skies. Similar to what they do in Pasadena. I asked how we didn't know that was still happening. She told me every region does this. It had been seen as an exercise in futility across the board, but definitely not a cause for concern. They had done a report on threat assessment. I was beginning to feel really out of the loop and didn't like it. I yelled that it wasn't one that the president or I saw! She said, "No, sir, I don't imagine it would have made it to your desk, as it was considered a benign activity."

That was hollow consolation, as it was now a big hairy deal. I asked Agent Roberts how the hell we were going to contain this and whether any of the other regions knew. She informed me they didn't have full intel on all regions, but it didn't appear any of them had detected anything. They were probably not likely to have encountered anything. None of them did regular sweeps of the full sky. They concentrated on the space directly above them, watching for falling debris. They weren't sure why it happened that Africa was scanning outside their zone. She said it was "uncommon" . . . and "unbelievably poor timing" for us, I noted.

*Poor timing, indeed. Any clue what they were planning to do with this information?*

SD: Not at that point. Agent Roberts presented me with two options: continue trying to gather intelligence, so we could determine how to approach them . . . *if* we approached them at all. Or we could go the direct method. I instructed her to see what we could find out through back channels first. It took us the better part of a day to comprehend what was happening, and *we* talked to the ship. They wouldn't have any clue what it was from a blip on a radar screen. If we were lucky, they would write it off as a fallen satellite. She did not seem to think we would be so lucky. She said with this being an uncommon occurrence—setting aside the likelihood of suspicion of other governments—simple curiosity would drive them to investigate it.

We covered our tracks quite well, but there was information to be had. It would take them a while to piece it all together, but she felt certain they would. How long it would take them to fully comprehend the implications was harder to guess. She informed me they were in the process of finalizing a plan for moving them to a safe house until we could determine a longer-term plan for what to do with them. Miramar was the most predictable place for them to be, and so it was good someone was thinking clearly enough to take action on that. I thanked her and asked her not to go forward with the extraction plan until we got the order from the president. I asked her to have something in writing for me on all they knew within the hour.

*Seems this was escalating quickly.*

SD: At an exponential rate, and I was not looking forward to delivering this news, but there was no time for stalling to feel better about things. We had to move immediately if we wanted to contain the situation.

*How did the president receive the news?*

SD: Well, they were waiting rather impatiently, and all eyes were on me as I walked back into the situation room. Even if I had wanted to, I was not doing a good job of hiding what was going on in my head. In fact, the president said as much. "General Dunne, your face says it all, but give it to us straight. We aren't in the clear, are we?" I had to tell her no—something you never want to have to tell the commander in chief. I explained that while we did not think they had any useful intel at this time, the African region was aware something came in from outer space. We definitely did not want to wait around for them to get it. I informed her Agent in Charge Samantha Roberts was preparing an extraction plan report. She asked if that wasn't . . . "a bit overly military." I spoke frankly and firmly with her, explaining, "Ma'am, if there is any chance others know of their presence, it's going to get *military* fast. They will not be secure where they are, and you can count on someone trying to get their hands on the crew. It won't take long for anyone with half a brain to figure out the implications." Her concern was that after so many years of peace, we could see that unravel if we made one misstep. She wanted to be sure we were taking the right measures to protect them without creating an international incident. I told her that was precisely why we needed to move them and keep this contained.

*You expected some sort of retaliation or armed insurgence?*

SD: "Well, I couldn't assure the president that the Africans were the only ones who knew, and while they may not have the resources for that type of action, there were others who did. We were continuing to gather intelligence as best we could without drawing attention, but we just didn't know anything for sure at that point. She ordered me to get sure. She didn't want any more surprises. Of course none of us did. I promised to keep her briefed as more information came in and once the team was ready to move. That is when she dismissed us and suggested we reconvene in two hours to discuss next steps. She asked us to stay close and keep this under wraps. No conversations outside secure channels. Unnecessarily overstating the obvious.

*Thank you, General Dunne. I know you have to attend to duties, but I would like to continue the conversation.*

*[General Dunne would offer more insight later, but it would not be the news I hoped to report.]*

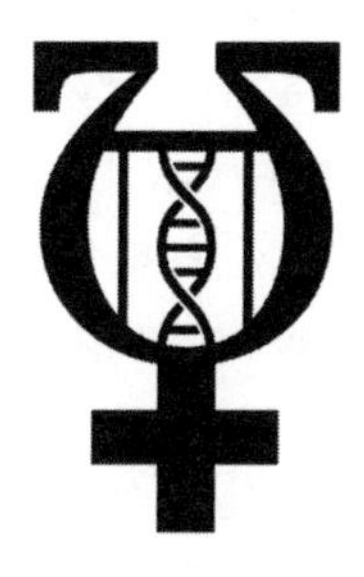

# CHAPTER EIGHT

## EXPLAINING THE UNEXPLAINABLE

*[Unfortunately, Captain Halverson was unavailable to speak with me, but I received the following letter sharing some of her reflections on her experience.]*

Initially I began this as an entry in my captain's log, but there's no point in making this official anymore. I'm not the captain of anything any longer. But I'll start with Day 1 of what I called the New World Order. We were rescued just a few short hours ago, and yet it feels like it's been a week since we came in for a crash landing. We were swept up from the ocean, hauled in a caravan, and secreted into a bunker, then tucked ever so neatly into what looks like a clinic, but feels like a cage. This tidal wave of information has come crashing over us and washed us away from the reality we thought existed.

I still can't believe that beautiful ship is gone. I can't believe everything I left is gone. I guess, to sum it up, I am in utter disbelief about everything at the moment. It's cliché, but I really do feel like I am in a nightmare and cannot wake up. People say that about their lives when they go through a divorce, financial ruin, the death of a loved one, or some other major life change they weren't expecting or prepared for. But this . . . this is something altogether different. This is (without hyperbole) a nightmare of epic proportions.

You know that list of the Top 100 Most Stressful Life Experiences? We checked off all of them and added a few. I am literally living out the stuff of science fiction, stuff you'd see in a movie and say, "That's pure fantasy. That could never happen." But it did happen. It is happening. It's all so surreal. We really should have seen some of this coming. Okay, maybe not the black hole, but then again, we were exploring the unknown parts of the universe. I guess running into a black hole wasn't totally implausible . . . but surviving it . . . that definitely was not something we expected.

When I told Lucas to go full bore into it, I was sure we were going to be ripped to shreds. I had a tiny sliver of hope that my crapshoot of an idea that it would be the "right" kind of black hole would pan out for us, but my confidence was really more for show. I did not expect it to work. I was totally putting on a brave face for the crew, trying to ease some of the fear going into their last minutes. It was an absolute, undeniable miracle that we survived this thing that has become the symbol of oblivion.

Or maybe we didn't and we really are dead, and I wasn't as good a person as I thought I was, and this is what hell looks like. Maybe I am damned. Also, it could be I was unplugged from one Matrix and plugged into another. I guess I can't really know, and I'm going to make myself crazy trying to figure it out. I guess that concussion is messing with my head more than I'd like to admit.

But, for just a moment, let's just assume we did survive and all of this is real. Setting aside all of the sci-fi, and considering what survival actually means, has its own mind-boggling implications. It definitely hasn't looked how we imagined. There was no heroes' parade welcoming us home, no fanfare, not even an acknowledgement we returned. Talk about anticlimactic.

Although, to be honest, I can't say we went through hell in the time we were gone. Yes, it was scary, and confusing, and unbelievable, but there wasn't what I would call a traumatic experience. Some of the crew might say different, but that's really being melodramatic. Once we woke up from the jolt . . . oh, yeah, that blackout when we went in was pretty weird, but we had no real sense of how long we were out. There were no instruments working to give us a clue about how much time had passed. Still, when we woke up, we felt fuzzy and discombobulated, but not traumatized. A couple of the crew members were sick from it, but nothing life-threatening. We did a wellness check of everyone and things seemed to be fine. We had no clue where we were . . . as I said, nothing was working, so we had no navigational system, and out in the expansive cosmos, it was hard to tell one star from another. It all looked the same. But we were okay and, recognizing the mission was a bust, were just focused on finding our way back home. We just drifted until we saw a larger celestial body that looked familiar. That's when we began to have hope for actually making it back home. My best guess is that we passed through a wormhole that dropped us back into our part of the solar system, just on the other side. Although it just as easily could have been the same location, but because the planets—hell, the whole universe—had forty years' worth of orbit to reposition themselves, it just looked different.

We probably will never know. I can't even begin to explain how we lost four decades in that wormhole or why we didn't age or even feel such a significant passage of time. And, to be honest, even more than the lost time, I'm saddened most by the fact that in the time we were gone, the space programs of the entire planet were lost as well. So we aren't likely going to be able to figure any of this out. Don't get me wrong, it is crushing me to think of the friends and family who have evaporated from my world, and some members of our crew are really having a hard time. We've barely been able to keep Kamil contained. If he were less scientific and more mechanical-oriented as an engineer, he probably would have tunneled his way out of the bunker before dinner. As it was, he raised plenty of hell. What most people don't know is that he was separated from his wife when he went on the mission. It was actually their cover for essentially divorcing without actually doing so, since their religion prohibits it. But can you imagine parting on bad terms from someone you love and having absolutely no hope of ever making it right? And we had a couple other crew members from our IT team who tried to hack the system where they were recording our evals to reach out to parents or siblings, and it ended up getting all of our movements restricted and scrutinized for the rest of the day. I doubt Abe, Hunter, and I will have to enforce any restrictions going forward because no one was happy about the total blackout. I have a feeling the rest of the crew will make sure no one steps out of line. They aren't going to let the whole suffer because of the actions of a few. I guess that's the upside of mob rule?

Anyway, as I was saying, don't get me wrong about where my priorities lie. I want us out of here so we can begin rebuilding our lives with whatever friends and family we have left. But the whole purpose of our mission—our raison d'être, what we put our lives and relationships down here on hold for—was to understand what's out there beyond what we can see and to expand our knowledge of the mysteries held in the unexplored. The idea that all of that was a waste because we can't even learn from what went wrong goes against all of my professional and personal sensibilities.

But here's what I/we do know: Black holes aren't all the same, and they don't exactly do what we thought they did. (Okay, that was more of a confirmation of what we already suspected.) There are more of them than we thought there were (or at least more are forming all the time). And time dilation is only part of the weirdness in space that completely deconstructs our concept of time and proves it is just a man-made framework that only serves our human attempts to control the uncontrollable.

Whew! That was kinda deep. I've never been overly philosophical, but this experience has challenged everything I thought I knew. I still believe in science fundamentally, but there is so much out there that science just does not have the capacity to explain . . . at least not yet, maybe not ever.

This has been one hell of a day, and with the exception of the little crash-induced nap I had, I can't recall the last time I slept for more than a couple of hours at a time. I definitely need to try to catch some z's to gear up for tomorrow. I have a feeling there's more to come that could knock us on our asses.

Day Three of the New World Order

They are giving us a break from the probing and prodding and information download today. It's been an exhausting couple of days and everyone on the team is showing the wear and tear. So here's what I've learned since returning. Well, it's what they've disclosed so far. I am sure there is a whole lot they are withholding. The world is in a really dire state. Kind of makes me think not making it to Proxima b was an even greater missed opportunity. It sounds like we could use a new home.

While there are some really positive changes that have come out of this, so much has been lost that made humanity really thrive. I'm not being uberfeminist here, but if women could have gained more power without an apocalypse, I think we could be better off. Considering the fact that with women in leadership, there haven't been the testosterone-fueled power grabs and violence, they have proved that world peace is possible. I think we've known for a long time that with different leadership we could achieve a lot of what we have claimed to want for our world. It's just unfortunate that there wasn't much of that world left by the time it happened. I still remember how that #metoo movement started moving the needle. Of course back then we didn't expect things to change that much, and those who did were seen as ideologues, who weren't being realistic. I'm sure there are downsides, and I have a feeling we will find out what they are as soon as they let us out of here. But it is nice to think about the earth and all of its inhabitants being nurtured for the first time in centuries.

But at such a cost! That's the real tragedy. I'm not so feminist that I don't see the value in the balance that comes from having both masculine and feminine sensibilities guiding us. It's not that innovation and exploration are uniquely masculine, but it's clear that self-preservation has superseded any risk-taking to find a solution. It is a very maternal instinct to seek shelter for protection rather than to attack a threat.

Here I am making really stereotypical statements, and I know my girlfriends in my professional group would eviscerate me if they could hear me . . . Wow. I just realized that many of them could be gone now. As much as I want out of here,

I'm not sure I want to go back home to find out what's left and what's not. It's almost better to have it remain an abstract idea instead of having losses confirmed.

Anyway, I know I'm perpetuating stereotypes, but they exist for a reason. The template fits most circumstances. But that's not an argument worth having right now. The point is, things are very different, and the lack of patriarchal religious systems on top of more peace-seeking governments has to be a good thing. I will admit to being really bummed about the idea of competitive sports being cast aside. I do think fostering a competitive spirit in a healthy way and cultivating national pride has many benefits, though I get why the economy wouldn't sustain it as a business. I just don't like it. I don't feel the loss over Hollywood the way a lot of people would. I never had time for TV and most of the movies they were making when we left were the same old, same old. My dad hated Hollywood for other reasons, being a small-town Conservative (with a capital C!), but I just wasn't motivated to fork over so much at the theater for something that seemed so recycled. But enough about that for now.

They really put us through the paces yesterday, even more than the first day. I didn't think there was anything left to test, but they found plenty of other ways to scour our bodies and minds for information. I was right about the troops keeping each other in line. Nobody wants to be subjected to such intensive isolation again, so they are being good little soldiers. I feel so powerless, which is not a comfortable place for me to sit at all, having been in charge of such an important project for nearly eighteen months before we even launched into space. I wasn't drunk on my power, but it's hard not to get a little full of self-importance at times. But now I can't do anything for my crew. I'm required to be as submissive as they are and I have no way to get the answers they are so desperately seeking. I don't get to give the orders anymore, and I definitely don't get to say with confidence that everything is under control.

I can't help but be really suspicious of everything they are doing. The men are enduring even more tests than the women. I understand there is a reproductive crisis, but something isn't sitting right with me. I can tell Hunter and Abe have formed some sort of two-man coalition and aren't keeping me in the loop. I am not comfortable with the tribalism that this suggests, but I get why they might feel the need to isolate. With women making up the majority of the power structure of the entire planet, it's no surprise that the men might not trust any female right now. Oh, how the tables have turned!

The biggest red flag for me at the moment is this vaccine. I know a lot has changed since we we've been gone, but that injection was unlike any I've ever had. But maybe it's just Hunter's Big Brother paranoia rubbing off on me. They informed us that they will be moving us to another facility tomorrow. Supposedly, it is for our comfort and security as we re-assimilate, but that doesn't feel right either. I mean, I get that none of us have homes any longer, so it makes sense for them to house us for now, and without a space exploration program, we're basically unemployed—actually, not just unemployed, but maybe unemployable—and so we aren't exactly in a position to just resume normal lives. Still, there is an element of . . . I guess . . . "containment" . . . is the word? I don't know. It's been a long couple of days. We'll see what develops tomorrow.

Day Four of the New World Order
I don't have much time. They are transporting us to our new "accommodations" and I'm not supposed to have this journal with me. If they see it, they will confiscate it and then I don't know when I'd be able to write more. Things definitely don't feel right though. We aren't going by normal transport. It isn't even a typical military escort. This is very covert. I recognize all the hallmarks of Special Ops draped over our movements and who is doing the moving. And moving twenty-six people secretly has to be a monumental undertaking. Of course Hunter is all over this, asking probing questions and getting more and more agitated by the minute. But he isn't getting any information. Well, as savvy as he is, he is probably picking up information out of the lack of information. I am going to confer with him when we can get a few minutes alone. Okay, that's all for now. I've pushed my luck as far as it will go, and things are moving quickly now.

# CHAPTER NINE
## AN ALIEN ABDUCTION

*Hunter, thank you for talking with me again. I'd like to skip ahead to the events surrounding your transport. There seem to be some conflicting reports. Can you clear up any of this?*

HY: Well, things didn't smell right from the start, and nothing I saw made me any less suspicious.

*How so?*

HY: It was a gut feeling mostly, but there was this: The thing is you can change the gender, but there are still very distinct markers of soldiers trained for special ops. All soldiers tend to carry themselves with a certain rigidity and cadence, and I don't think that really goes away, but there is a stoicism, a no-nonsense essence in those who have to execute missions with precision and swiftness under unpredictably volatile circumstances. They—whoever was running the show—wanted us to believe this was a standard transport team and that all of these precautions were just normal security protocol. I knew better. For one thing, the heavy artillery alone (which they thought we hadn't noticed) was a dead giveaway. Then there was the need-to-know nature of how information was flowing. And who wouldn't be suspicious of all the code they used to speak to one another?

*So just those observations raised your antennas?*

HY: Even a civilian would have thought it was a bit odd, but, sure, being ex-military myself, I saw all kinds of red flags. Abe was finally tracking with me, but we hadn't read in the captain yet. It's not that we didn't trust her—we just didn't trust anyone else—and we hadn't had the opportunity for any private conversations that wouldn't raise suspicions. At the first facility Abe and I were able to talk under cover of our shared quarters. But with the women basically sequestered from the men, conferring with Sonja had been nearly impossible. Once they put us in armored, blacked-out vehicles, so they could whisk us away to who knows where, and we were in earshot of our captors, any covert communication was out the window. And, yes, I mean *captors.* I wasn't buying for one second that this whole scenario was for our protection and well-being any longer. Major Statham was right. I shouldn't have been so quick to dismiss her just because she was being ambiguous. This all actually felt very sinister.

*Did they tell you where you were headed?*

HY: You're kidding, right?

*I guess not. Were you able to figure out from any landmarks or anything where you might be going?*

HY: Not having watches, or phones, or any other device for determining time or anything else that might have given us a clue about where we were, I was only guessing, but I figured we'd been on the road for about an hour, headed northeast when we stopped. Although, for all I know, we could have been going southwest. I got a basic directional feel as we left the facility based on the sun's position, but we took so many turns (I think that was intentional to throw us off), I may have lost track. All the same, based on the direction I thought we were heading, and the long stretches of dry desolation that reached in every direction, I was guessing our next destination would have been Dulce Base. Wouldn't that have been ironic? Treating us like a bunch of aliens that dropped out of the sky.

*Why is that?*

HY: It is . . . or was . . . a secure site, and probably the closest of its kind, but it was a less publicized version of Area 51! I guess it made sense to put us there. And maybe I just made myself eligible for the tinfoil-hat brigade, but I doubt anyone would be so critical of my suspicion considering what we know now. Looking back, I realize that was a really long way to go by ground. I suppose they could have been taking us to an airfield to fly the rest of the way to wherever we were going. Although flying would have immediately put us on literal and figurative radars that, I sense, they didn't want us to be on. So, while it was less expedient, surface travel (in theory) would have drawn less attention. The only trick was that pit stops, like the one we were taking when everything went down, were necessary for such a long road trip, and they posed a few challenges of their own. Maybe they were counting on the fact that we were basically traveling through barren desert country. Tiny, hole-in-the-wall gas station/diner stops; quiet, remote Podunk towns, Population: 15; and the apparent collapse of far-reaching telecommunication provided good cover for them, I suppose. They told us in the briefings that the internet and mobile coverage were a shadow of their former selves, but I had a hard time fathoming that, what with how dependent we had become on those tools. And yet, each time we stopped along the way, I noticed something that didn't register fully until now: I could see the faces of the people we encountered. They weren't head down, enthralled by a screen in their hands. It's a condition we had become so accustomed to that not seeing it was noteworthy.

*That's pretty common these days, but I can see how it would have been odd for you.*

HY: Still, the team moved with the military-like precision they were trained for as we pulled in to take care of business. The driver stayed behind the wheel, while another guard took care of fueling the vehicle, and the other soldier assigned to our group hustled those of us who needed to relieve ourselves into the small, ramshackle building. No refreshments. Strict orders. It just meant more stops. Abe and I decided to stay behind and take advantage of the brief opportunity for privacy. I heard this muffled "Hntr. Hntr." Then I felt an elbow in my ribs as I was about to get up to let Li and Kamil out of the backseats. It took a minute for me to realize that the mumbling was supposed to be my name.

Abe is about as subtle as a neon sign. He said something felt really off about all of this. Thankfully, he had abandoned the attempts to talk through his teeth and was now just whispering. But he still piqued the interest of the other passengers, and I really couldn't risk getting them all worked up. I said, "I think you've just been sitting too long. Maybe you should stretch your legs." I climbed out in a poorly veiled attempt to deflect, so we could get rid of our audience. Abe followed me, but, thankfully, the rest of our group was called more by nature than their desire to know what was up, so they headed to the can. We moved slowly toward the building, as if we had the same destination, and I turned to Abe with the calmest look I could muster and said through a strained smile, "No shit, things are off. You're just now picking that up?"

*Did you expect him to be as quick as you were on these details? He wasn't trained for that, like you were.*

HY: Yeah, I just thought we were on the same page by now. He said he was not as wary by nature as I am, which is a fair assessment, but he said he did feel it when they loaded us in the vehicles and he was getting really worried. He asked if I noticed the way each of the vehicles parked—catty-cornered at the pumps. Of course I had.

*What does that mean?*

HY: It's strategic maneuvering to guard against a vehicle interdiction. They are positioned that way to avoid being blocked in, in case there is need for a hasty exit.

*And that's what you saw?*

HY: Yeah. It might not register with anyone not looking for an excuse to be suspicious. With multiple SUVs at the pumps, it could have been seen as just a way to get them all in there at once. But, for me, it was just further confirmation that nothing was "standard" or "normal," and I didn't like it at all. I also didn't like the fact that I didn't notice first. I guess I was too busy worrying about what might be coming and overlooked what was happening. I told myself I needed to get my head in the game and pay closer attention . . . like the major said. Man, I wish I'd not been so arrogant and impatient with her.

*I guess you owe her an apology . . . and a thank-you.*

HY: If I see her again, you can bet I will. But she was gone when they loaded us up that day. Nowhere to be seen. I hate to think what may have happened to her.

*We spoke with her by phone shortly before you were moved, but have been unable to reach her since. None of this sounds good for her.*

HY: No. No, it does not. But I had other things to worry about in the moment.

*Such as?*

HY: The driver stayed in the vehicle too.

*Okay, you're going to have to explain that to me as well. I'm not versed in clandestine ops. What did* that *tell you?*

HY: Again, for a hasty exit. The spot where a driver sits is the best-protected spot in an armored vehicle.

*How do you know all of this? I read your bio and know you were in the Air Force, but did you learn all of this just to fly planes?*

HY: Some of it, yeah. As Abe and I were standing around talking about everything he was noticing, I did some noticing of my own and saw a guard approaching us. I'm guessing they didn't like the fact that we were standing around out in the open, so I carefully took Abe's arm and nudged him toward the building as we continued talking. I told him I didn't know what we were up against, but I knew we needed to keep our eyes peeled. The guards with us knew what they were doing, but we still would all be better off if we weren't doing anything dumb to make their jobs harder. Abe said he got that, but asked me, honestly, what did I expect to happen. I just said, "Anything, Abe. Anything." And no sooner had those words left my mouth than six SUVs, seemingly out of nowhere, swept in and formed a barricade. The tiny lot surrounding the gas station was suddenly overrun by a fleet of dark transportation, and the air around us was hot enough to ignite a catastrophic flame. Our guards flew into action, trying to secure those of our group who went inside and to lock down the vehicles. M-4s materialized in the hands of every one of our soldiers in the vicinity, and what happened next was right out of any big-budget Hollywood action flick.

*That sounds terrifying. What happened?*

HY: A team piled out of each of the vehicles surrounding us, spraying bullets that pinged off the side of our vehicle and left divots in the windows.

*Seriously? Was anyone hurt?*

HY: Not then, and it oddly gave me some reassurance.

*You must be joking.*

HY: Not exactly. I mean, had we been in the vehicles, it was clear we would have been safe because the bullets didn't penetrate. But they seemed to have an endless supply of ammo they were intent on spending entirely on us. I saw them approaching the vehicles, and I did not want Abe to see what I knew was coming next, so I pulled him to the ground, telling him to duck. But, honestly, it wouldn't have mattered if our self-preservation instinct had failed us. Because even as our faces met the pavement, we felt the thud of a body falling on top of us, and a forceful "Stay down" resounded in our ears.

*Was that one of the guards?*

HY: Yes, she didn't waste any time putting herself between us and the threat . . . as she was trained to do. The rain of fire showered over us as these insurgents moved in on the drivers, dragged them from their positions, and, in a bloody show of force, took them out.

*Oh, no! They killed them?! That wasn't reported.*

HY: It wouldn't be. The public doesn't get body counts or other details on a dark mission like this. But, our guards returned in full measure, and bodies were dropping all around us. It was an all-out massacre, but none of them were civilian casualties. I did not suppose this was a stroke of luck for us. As morbid as it sounds, it was clearly a surgical strike, with impressive precision.

*That does sound morbid. It almost seems like you . . . admire them?*

HY: What can I say? I may not like what they did, but I can appreciate the expertise in which they did it. Anyway, when they had finished emptying their guns (or so I thought), the assailants emerged from their own cover and surrounded us with their weapons trained on us. Though, actually, now that I think about it, it's more accurate to say they were pointed at our soldiers, and very purposefully not targeting us. Those remaining were instructed, with as few words as possible, to get up and hand over their weapons, and then to lie facedown in a row. I was more terrified for these young women who seemed to be assembled in a firing line than for the safety of our crew. I shuddered at the thought of what was in store. It was gruesome, but it was not out of the ordinary for battle, and that is clearly what was unfolding around us.

*I cannot imagine.*

HY: That's a good thing. I wish the members of our crew who had gone inside the building when the siege began hadn't seen any of it. They wisely sheltered in place, but were being horded out into the parking lot by a couple of the mysterious . . . I would have to say they were soldiers as well, but definitely not American.

*How do you know that?*

HY: Well, they didn't speak much, which I assume was to minimize the identification of an accent, but they definitely had military training from somewhere. But it was obvious, anyway, from the fragments I heard that there was a hint of an accent that was very much *not* American.

*Any idea from where?*

HY: Who knows? Mercenaries, maybe? An opposing government? The thing is, I thought there was supposed to be a more peaceful way of life now. I was full of more questions . . . as if I didn't have enough already. But there was no time to explore them. After they had us all gathered and accounted for, they loaded us into their vehicles. They did it more gently than I would have imagined during an abduction, but still with enough force that they communicated clearly how unwise it would be to resist. As we rolled out, the terror-filled silence that hung over all of us in the vehicle I was in (and I assume in the others as well) was shattered by the echoing of gunshots that followed us out of the lot and down the road. No one dared look back. We didn't need to. We knew what it meant.

*I think I know too. Let's move on. What did they do with you?*

HY: The next few hours were a blur of movement, stern silence, and muffled grief. Somehow we knew our lives weren't in danger, and yet we were terrified all the same. The sense of foreboding was palpable as they shuffled us into the belly of a small cargo plane. Even though we had not had enough time to become accustomed to this New World Order we were told about, we knew this was a big departure from the status quo, and it was not a good sign. We knew enough to get that this action was going to change everything, and it would bring back a lot of the conflict and dysfunction that had apparently subsided in the wake of the pandemic. What we didn't know was how exactly we fit into all of it. It was pretty obvious our return stirred up all kinds of issues, and I'm pretty sure there were some kind of plans for us in the works, but I didn't really have a grasp at the time of what it all meant for us.

*Where did the plane take you?*

HY: Based on how long our excursion took, I put together a reasonable suspicion that we were no longer in the US . . . or whatever they are calling it these days. We were locked away in yet another dungeon of sorts. This one definitely was not maintained as well as the other, and our new captors were taking fewer precautions about masking their accents. They were clearly Russian, although I also heard a few others that sounded almost British, but I later figured out these were South Africans. Though we were sequestered in cells, the drafty, crumbling walls allowed a lot of sound to penetrate. I couldn't see them, but I could tell when the Russians were talking among themselves, and when the South Africans were having private conversations of their own, because they were using their native languages. When they were communicating with each other, they used surprisingly good English. I wasn't sure, but it seemed as though they weren't aware this place wasn't soundproof, because they weren't especially guarded about what they said in English, unless they just weren't concerned about being overheard.

*What did you overhear? Did it give you any insight about what was happening?*

HY: From what I was able to piece together, they didn't really know what to do with us. They just wanted to get us away from American control. The plan for the abduction was thrown together and executed quickly, but the decisions about what to do with us once they had possession of us were still under debate. I wasn't sure if this was a side effect of a women-led military or just being rusty from lack of use, but there did not seem to be a lot of strategy employed.

*Really? You may need to rethink some of the things that just tumble out of your mouth because, I can promise you, that's not an attitude that will get you very far in this era.*

HY: Yeah, I know how that sounds, and I don't mean to come off as a pig. Hell, I served under a female captain, but the reality is there are primarily women in power now, so it's a fair observation. To their credit, if they have not had any need for military incursions for the last twenty years, that is quite an accomplishment. But that is exactly what got me wondering even more, why now? Why us? What did they want with us, and why did it warrant such an aggressive maneuver?

*Fair enough. Obviously, as you said, the public doesn't get information about these sorts of missions, but for those of us with an ear to the underground, there still hasn't been much indication of such action. What happened next?*

HY: They didn't have us separated, as we were at Miramar. We were all in one large room with decaying plaster walls and no windows, huddled on dingy mattresses, shivering in the bone-chilling cold that was typical of far-northern climates. And that, paired with the predominance of Russian accents, supported my theory that we were probably somewhere in Eastern Europe, or whatever it's called now in the new configuration—I guess I am looking at a world-geography refresher course at some point. I hated geography. Anyway, the slop they dumped into bowls and shoved in front of us also held big clues, not only about our location, but the lack of preparation involved as well. Abe was settled in next to Sarah on a mattress adjacent to mine, attempting to comfort her and communicating loads to me with very quick, but expressive, glances in my direction. When our eyes met, it just confirmed we were on the same page, and it wasn't a good one. We both scanned the room and then met back up to communicate our concern nonverbally. Our team was traumatized, as if they hadn't already been through more than enough in the last week. And, if I know Sonja . . . and I do, very well . . . what I was reading on her face was a deep, internal battle to deal with her own fear, while trying to figure out how to lead when she didn't even have the semblance of control. She brought us through an unimaginable crisis virtually unscathed, so I was sure she was asking herself how she could manage that and let us end up stolen and secreted away to some dank hole in a godforsaken land of destitution. Yeah, I'm editorializing, but I know how she thinks, which is really similar to the way I do, and that's exactly what I'd be thinking.

*I can see how that would be a tough position for a leader to be in.*

HY: Yeah. The rest of our crew just looked exhausted, confused, and a lot worse for wear than when we left Miramar. And I didn't have any more of a clue of what to say to ease their minds than Sonja did. Lucas leaned over to me at one point and asked what the hell was going on. All I could say was that his guess was as good as mine. Then he said something that kind of just gut-punched me. He said, "Well, you were outside when all of this went down. I kind of got caught with my you know what in my hand . . . literally. I was taking a leak when I heard what sounded like fireworks going off outside." Can you imagine being in such a vulnerable state when the world comes crashing down?

*No, I can't. I hope never to find out.*

HY: Same here. I told him that all I knew was a team of people descended on us like a pack of ninjas—totally out of nowhere—and before we had time to think, we were swept up and our transport team was disabled. He asked the obvious question, "No one saw this coming?"

*Yes, that does seem like an obvious question. And no one did?*

HY: It didn't seem so. I know they were taking every precaution to keep this on the down low, but something tells me they weren't aware anyone else knew about us.

*How is that possible?*

HY: I don't know, but then, there is so much we still don't know. Lucas looked like he was about to ask me something else, but almost as a re-play of what happened at the gas station, an explosion of gunfire and shouting echoed down the corridors outside our cell.

*That's when you were retrieved and brought back, correct?*

HY: Yeah. But it's definitely not the end of the drama by a long shot.

# CHAPTER TEN
## RESCUED?

*General, when we last talked, you had just learned the South Africans knew about the return of the* Alpha Centauri *crew, but you were moving them to a safer location. What exactly happened?*

SD: What a shit show. We were in the process of trying to figure all of that out when we were blindsided. Scrambling to clean this up was equally a nightmare. So much at stake.

*That's a colossal understatement.*

SD: With far-reaching ramifications. We scrambled to put a team together to go in and rescue them. I was hoping to have some good news to deliver in real time when President Marshall joined us in the situation room for a briefing. I knew she was not going to want to hear any excuses. I asked Agent Roberts what the hell went wrong. She told me the more recent intel indicated that the South Africans discovered the Russians knew about the return of the *Alpha Centauri* team as well—our worst-case scenario coming true. The South Africans alone did not have the resources to execute a covert op like this in such an expeditious and strategic way. They needed outside help and, clearly, the Russians were all too happy to oblige.

*How exactly did the Russians get involved?*

SD: Well, I'm sure you know they have a long history of spy craft that rivals our own, which isn't exactly a surprise. But their wading into, much less instigating, this mess was unforeseen.

*Did the Africans clue them in, or did they know in advance? And if they did, why weren't we aware of it?*

SD: Honestly, we have had little reason to believe they were still active, considering the lack of military conflict for the last two decades. They were hit as hard as the African nations were by the pandemic. Our best guess is the Africans approached them for tactical support in their plans to seize the team.

*Our intelligence team didn't pick up on this?*

SD: Precisely the question I wanted answered, because I knew I would be accounting for it with the president. But at the moment our focus was on retrieval of the team, and I wanted a rundown of our options before President Marshall showed up. I couldn't have her walking in while we had our . . . um . . . were not prepared. Unfortunately, she came in just as Agent Roberts was starting to brief me, so I still got an earful.

*What was the plan?*
SD: We had a team in overwatch, awaiting her command to move on the compound.

Compound? *Sounds like they were in for a real fight.*

SD: Well, that was a generous term . . . They were being held in an old bunker near Belarus. The people who took them clearly did not have time to prepare a more secure location, so we anticipated that extraction would be fairly simple.

*So this was pulled off by a half-assed band of screwups?*

SD: No, they were well-trained soldiers, and our team was caught off guard. It's just whoever planned this, and sent them after the crew, didn't seem to think much beyond the abduction.

*Wait. How did they catch our* guards *"off guard"? Wasn't that kind of their one job?*

SD: Don't misunderstand me. It was very much a "shock and awe" type of maneuver, and our team was focused on expediting a rest stop. Their orders were to keep the crew alive at all costs. In that, the mission was not a failure. President Marshall didn't quite see it that way. She still called it a failure, but she granted that at least we didn't lose any of the civilians. We lost more than a dozen valued soldiers, which was a tragedy, but she said they weren't our priority at that point. She promised there would be an accounting, to be sure, but our focus had to be getting the crew back.

*So, what was your next move?*

SD: Agent Roberts told President Marshall that on her word the team we had moved into place would breach the entrances and gather the crew. We had secured two decommissioned helos to transport them to an airfield where they would be loaded onto a fixed-wing craft and brought back to Langley.

*I guess that meant your secret was out.*

SD: Yeah, well, there definitely was no putting that toothpaste back in the tube.

*Was President Marshall ready to give the go-ahead then?*

SD: Well, there was a hell of a lot that could go wrong. And since we no longer had the element of surprise, there was concern about more casualties. And we couldn't rule out the possibility of more attempts at interception, once we had them back in our possession, so she wanted to know what contingencies we had gamed out. Our primary goal at the time was to get them safely back to our turf. We knew they would be expecting us, though not likely this soon.

*Why is that?*

SD: Well, this is going to have to come under that off-the-record agreement we had earlier. It will come out eventually, but it can't go public right now.

*Of course. None of our discussion will be revealed until after you leave the administration.*

SD: Seriously, I'm relying on your journalistic integrity here. That doesn't hold a lot of water for most people anymore, but I'm trusting you to do the right thing.

*General, you have my word. What is this about?*

SD: They . . . the Russians and the South Africans . . . didn't know we had already tracked them.

*How did you do that?*

SD: The chips that were inserted with the vaccines . . .

*I'm sorry. What* chips*? Which* vaccine*?*

*[Sighing heavily, he shifted in his seat, and I knew at this point I was about to get the scoop of a lifetime.]*

SD: All of the pandemic vaccines included a microchip implant. Everyone got one . . . at least everyone who received a vaccine from the Americas.

*That's a joke, right? I mean, you can't mean you seriously did that.*

SD: Look, I'm just the messenger. But, yes, I am quite serious. The purpose behind it was to be able to monitor the spread of the infection, to know who was inoculated against it, and who they were mating with, in the hopes that we could contain the spread.

*General, do you understand what you've just admitted to?*

SD: Again, just the messenger. I was not involved in that. In fact, I was just a grunt in those days. I know it is earth-shattering news, but that's not the most germane part of the discussion right now. The point is, those chips also went into the crew when they got the vaccines at Miramar, and that allowed us to get a lock on their location quickly and get our forces in position soon after they arrived at the bunker.

*I guess you could use that as one argument in favor of this gross violation of privacy.*

SD: Agreed, but we had been chipping our people this way since the plague started. People with a higher pay grade than mine, many years before I even had the ear of decision makers, had a long list of reasons they considered it a necessary evil. Fortunately, this practice was not common knowledge, so it worked in our favor—also a point for those of us who were still going to catch hell for the snafu of losing them in the first place. So the plan was that we would ask the team to perform one final recon report, and then they would be ready to move when the president was. She told us to do it and Agent Roberts pressed a button on a comm sitting in the middle of the table and said, "Bravo One . . . sit rep." That's when the disembodied voice of a young woman, who couldn't have been more than twenty years old, spoke in the clipped and concise manner of a soldier reporting from the front lines, informing us, "Ground sniper counts two hostiles at front, one at back. ISR registers multiple signatures through infrared. Most are clustered 91 meters east of primary point of entry. Six more are stationary along corridor." Roberts told her to stand by for orders and then turned to President Marshall, looking for a response. The president said, "Tell them to go get our astronauts back." And Roberts told her we would experience a momentary blackout, once they executed.

*Sorry, what's ISR?*

SD: I forget I'm talking to a civilian. Intelligence, surveillance, and reconnaissance.

*Got it. And you were all in the situation room at this point? I've always wondered what it looks like in there.*

SD: It's just a room, really. The only difference is what goes on in there. You don't have to run an op from there, but it is the most secure location, and it was where we were linked in with the team on the ground. There were multiple screens consuming one wall of the room that revealed views of the bunker from body cams, as well as infrared and thermal drone broadcasts and monitoring from ground-force command positions.

*Was it like in war movies?*

SD: Not exactly. It's far less dramatic than what they give you for entertainment. I will say, I have seen a few movies and TV shows that got pretty close to the mark when they portray scenes like the one I was watching. The thing is, we aren't just shootin' the shit in there. Actions that impact people's lives in profound ways are ordered from in there. It isn't all the hysteria and pyrotechnics you might imagine, but they don't get just how tense things really are or how torturous the silences feel when you are waiting to hear from them.

*So they weren't communicating. Could you see anything?*

SD: Not a lot. The images from the body cams were shadowed in green and gray hues from the passive or night vision lens, and the frame was unsteady as the people wearing them were moving into position. I've only seen one other op broadcast this way, as we have done little in this regard since my early years of service. I was in the field at the time, watching it on a tiny monitor from base camp. Once we got the all clear, Agent Roberts asked the president to give the order. Somberly, but with a bit of eagerness, she nodded, and then said, "Go." Agent Roberts relayed the order, and moments later we heard a forceful but feminine voice over the comm.

*What do they say?*

SD: Well, they don't call each other by names. They have call signs. *Bravo One to Bravo Two*, that sort of thing. And then they relay positions and observations.

*I have the transcript here.*

SD: How did you get that?

*General, you are not my only source.*

SD: Then why do you need me?

*I need a high-ranking official like you to corroborate and fill in details. May I read you the transcript?*

SD: Go ahead.

*Okay, the first party . . . Bravo One says:*

*"Two hostiles at point of entry. Two signatures on the other side of the threshold. Four more positioned at intervals 40 and 90 meters east."*

*Then Bravo Two says:*

*"Roger. Are we clear to breach?"*

*Bravo One responds:*

*"Affirmative Two. Hostages are likely being held beyond a door where secondary guards are positioned. Proceed with caution. Bravo Four, one hostile on your end. Get ready to infiltrate from the rear."*

*Bravo Two confirms:*

*"Roger. Moving in."*

SD: Well, that sounds accurate, but they are just words on a page. You can't compare them to the impact of hearing those words from . . . Look, those were real people out there with real fear and even more real resolve in their voices. You just won't get it without hearing the rustle as they run forward, the heavy breathing, the unmistakable click of a gun being lifted into position. And then the muffled *pops* that don't quite sound as lethal as they are. You can hear the bodies drop and it is completely surreal. Then, once the camera stops bouncing, you see it—the sight that shocks even me—spirals of breath in the cold air that come to an abrupt stop as the figure in front of you exhales for the last time. What ensued was a frenzied jumble of shots fired, running, blows landed in hand-to-hand, more running, and then more shooting. The flashes of light from bullets leaving guns, and under-gun lights bobbing up and down, added to the confusion. Even with eyes on the scene from several angles, it was nearly impossible to determine what was going on.

*I don't know. It sounds way more dramatic than on TV to hear you tell it.*

SD: Only because it's real. Knowing they aren't actors who get up when the director yells "cut" has a different effect on you. With these people you aren't going to see them on another show next week. They are really gone. That is a sobering fact I hope I never lose in all of the intrigue.

*Thank you, General. Those are profound thoughts. How long did this last?*

SD: Not long. One soldier wearing a body cam followed two others who busted open a door to a large room and the harsh, narrow beam of their under-gun lights fell on terrified but familiar faces. As the comms came back online, we heard the soldier reassuring the clearly traumatized, but apparently unharmed, team that they were safe now, saying, "Ladies and gentlemen, everything is under control. Come with us and we'll get you to safety." As they began rounding them up, we could still hear ongoing clamor in the background as the rest of the extraction team cleaned up.

*What do you mean when you say "cleaned up"?*

SD: I think you know.

*Oh.*

SD: This is war. You don't leave people around to shoot you in the back as you are getting the hell out of Dodge. And they had to move the crew quickly out of the building to the helos that were approaching. They wouldn't have long to get everyone loaded and get out of there. And that's what they did. They didn't have time to be gentle, and they were all but dragging everyone on board when the exact scenario I just said you want to avoid actually happened.

*What do you mean?*

SD: If you have never had to get into a helicopter with rotors already in motion, you have no idea what a sensory overload it is to run through swirling debris toward enormous blades whirring rapidly just above your head. No matter how much you duck, you still fear they will take your head off, and it's easy to get disoriented. And that's what seems to have happened with one of the young crew members who froze halfway between the bunker and the transport. One of the soldiers wearing a body cam turned back for him just as two Russians emerged from the doorway, stumbling and fumbling with their rifles. Shots were fired from behind and they fell, but not before they got off a few rounds of their own.

*Why would they . . . That wasn't in the report.*

SD: We had to keep it under wraps. Guess your other source has access to only so much. We all shouted in disbelief . . . in unison. Since the op began, not a sound had been uttered in that room that seemed like a place where powerful people sit, yet there we were, helpless to change anything unfolding before us. I'm not sure any of us had even allowed a breath before that moment, as if holding our collective breaths might have helped things stay together.

*It must have been devastating to watch that and not be able to do anything to stop it.*

SD: You have no idea. We could not fathom what they just did. President Marshall cried, "Don't they have any idea what that life is worth?" I said, "Ma'am, I don't think they were aiming for him. Not that it makes a difference." She said it *most definitely* did make a difference. She called it "recklessness" and a "loss we couldn't afford."

*I know any loss of life is a tragedy, but her reaction seems . . . a bit overwrought.*

SD: A point I made to her. She said that young man represented an immeasurable amount of potential life. Then she said they had to do whatever was necessary to keep him alive until we could get him back and see what we could salvage.

*Salvage? That seems like an odd way to talk about saving his life.*

SD: I told her they obviously would not leave him behind. That's not what she meant.

*Oh, I think I'm going to be sick.*

SD: That is precisely how I felt, and I have had to stomach a lot, being in the military and with much of what we've had to do for survival since the pandemic. But this . . . this talk of harvesting bodily fluids from a young man stopped in his tracks before his life really began was just a bridge too far, and I feared what was on the other side was going to be even more inconceivable.

*How has President Marshall justified this? How does she plan to answer to the citizens of the Americas . . . of the world?*

SD: I don't mean to vilify her. She is making decisions for the greater good that most people are too weak to handle.

*Come on, General. Don't go soft on me now. I know you can't find any justification for this. You wouldn't be here talking to me if you did.*

SD: Look, this is unsavory for many reasons, but, as President Marshall knows, this is the distasteful reality of our world. I don't have to like it. I can't change it, and I definitely don't know of a better way. No, I don't know how much more of this I can tolerate, which is why I am leaving the administration, but I don't envy her the responsibility that rests on her shoulders. The "greater good" argument has been growing really thin for me, which makes it impossible for me to advise her well, so I am stepping down to make room for someone who can.

*When will that happen?*

SD: As soon as the crew is settled in a new location, and I can hand the reins of my duties over to someone she chooses. Roberts informed us a few minutes after the young man was shot that they were in the air and heading to the rendezvous point.

*What happened after that?*

SD: They went dark again until they made the handoff. Then we received a brief confirmation, and then there was continued radio silence until they made it back to our airspace. With nothing else to do there, President Marshall and I went back to the Oval until we could meet with the cabinet to determine how to proceed, once they were in custody again.

*Is that when you tendered your resignation?*

SD: Yes. Yesterday was my last day.

# CHAPTER ELEVEN
## GOD ONLY KNOWS

*[Unfortunately, this was the last communication I received from Captain Halverson. I received word of her passing a few days after this last letter. The circumstances of her death are unclear at this time. If I receive any further information, I will include an update in postproduction.]*

Where do I even start? In the last week we have emerged from a black hole, having traversed unknown parts of the universe, been poked and prodded like lab rats, shuttled into a caravan headed for an unknown destination, intercepted while on a potty break, whisked away to a crumbling hovel on the other side of the globe, snatched out of there and brought back to another compound. And except for the selectively doled-out briefs on what's fallen apart in our forty-year absence, we have no idea what's happening.

Hunter is the only one who seems to have any sense of what might be going on, and under any other circumstances I would have dismissed his theories as delusional and paranoid. I could not fathom, even in my most fantastical musings, that I would experience what has unfolded since I agreed to captain this expedition. The most radical and outlandish thing I could come up with was encountering sentient beings on Proxima b. And even that stretched my imagination to its furthest capabilities.

The "Americans" have us back in custody and under heavy guard. It is very clear they aren't taking any more chances with us, but it doesn't offer me any comfort. It does not feel as though their intentions are entirely honorable. At least the food is better.

I haven't even begun to process the loss of Harris. I was already on the helicopter and watched it happen without any way of doing anything about it. Could I have done anything? I don't know, but I am his captain and I should have been with him. He froze. He was terrified. Of course he was. It was a whirlwind of madness on top of a whirlwind of madness. I am grateful they took the risk to retrieve him and not leave him behind, but traveling with him as the life drained out of his body for so many hours was devastating for all of us. No one uttered a word the whole time. It was as if saying anything at all might hasten his final breath. Although, what can you say? We lost one of our own and it was senseless and cruel. We came through so much to get back here, only to have him cut down in the prime of his life. He had made so many sacrifices for his country, for the world, and didn't even have a chance to find love, get married, and have children. I know this is not unusual for those who choose to go into service, but he was about to have the opportunity for that, and in a split second that was taken away from him.

But there is no time for grieving now. We have to focus on what is next for us. We have to figure out what they are planning to do with us. We haven't even had a chance to contact any remaining family or friends . . . or to grieve any losses there. I don't know if my mother is still alive. Damn it! How is this right or fair?!

Whew! I guess that was building up for a while. I am a pretty pragmatic, grounded, and nonreactionary person. It's part of why I got the job I had. But this is too much to ask of a person.

If I believed in God before this, I'd certainly be questioning that belief now. How much is one person expected to endure? So much given with one hand, and so much taken away with the other before we ever had a chance to really hold it and enjoy it. I just don't understand.

I had the opportunity few in the history of humanity have had—to travel the vast expanse of the universe, to explore the unknown. There are so many mysteries about the darkness beyond the light of our sun. We took on one of the biggest that almost assuredly promised death, and we survived. I still can't quite wrap my brain around that. There are some astrophysics that might explain our journey, but this isn't exactly my wheelhouse, even though you'd think it would be, considering I am an ASTRONaut. But my job was more about being a pilot and knowing how to navigate wide-open spaces in a massive machine than explaining how that wide-open space operates.

But, I have been thinking a bit more about what might have happened from my limited understanding of the science. Einstein seemed to comprehend the incomprehensible basics of how traveling near the speed of light works. It's thanks to him that we managed to get into outer space at all. And his theories on relativity make for some intellectual acrobatics that are hard to get your brain around under normal circumstances, much less those we've been under. But the idea that time, in particular, is relative, and that the same moment experienced in different places can feel different as far as duration . . . that is what I'm trying to process to explain how we lost forty years in what was effectively the span of an afternoon nap. I don't know if this holds up scientifically, but the way I think about it is like when you come home from work and talk to your partner about their day and you say, "Today just dragged on for me. It felt like it would never end;" but, they say, "Oh, it flew by for me. I looked up and it was already afternoon." You both had the same eight-ish hours at the office, but for one of you it felt like two days-worth, and the other like half a day. As I said, the relativity Einstein was talking about may not apply, as it involves much more complicated concepts around mass and movement, but the idea that everything is relative does.

At any rate, it's too much to unpack with my limited knowledge and what we've endured since we got back. Right now I'm more concerned about where our future is going than where our past went. We are supposed to get another download of information soon, though I don't really think they are going to tell us everything they could . . . like who took us and why, what they plan to do with us now, when we can see something other than bunkers and the inside of transport vehicles, and, most important, and what seems to have been hopelessly lost in the shuffle—when we will get to communicate with our loved ones.

*****

They assembled us a little while ago and we sat waiting for nearly thirty minutes for some official to come talk to us. Hunter, not surprisingly, was twitchy and impatient. But the whole crew seemed to have risen to his level of agitation as well. These people who are holding us are sitting on a powder keg, and I don't think they have any idea just how bad it's about to get. I did not envy the woman who walked into this mess. A different face. I guess they opted for sending a new lamb to slaughter. A variety of people stood before us making empty promises about our safety and false assurances that we would have all the information we wanted soon. I guess none of them had any desire to answer to us now. I did notice Hunter seems to be overly concerned about what happened to Major Statham, the last person in this position. Not sure what that's about. I made a mental note to explore that with him later. In the meantime I just focused on what this messenger had to say.

She began with, "Ladies and gentlemen, if I could have your attention, please." And, boy, she had it, alright. There was not a single pair of eyes not boring holes through her, waiting for her to start talking.

She said, "I know you've been through quite an ordeal, and President Marshall has asked me to convey her regrets for what has happened and her deepest condolences for the loss of your colleague and friend."

Hunter's lid absolutely came off and he exploded, asking why she wasn't here talking to us if that was true. Why did she send a lackey if she was all that torn up about it? Leave it to him to say what we are all thinking in a way we wouldn't have the balls to say it.

Again, I don't envy this girl. She really was such a young thing tasked with some really difficult responsibilities. She tried to be sympathetic talking about how she knew tensions were running high and we were understandably distressed about what we'd experienced in the last couple of days. She asked for cooler heads to prevail. Ha! That ship sailed some time ago, as Hunter was quick to remind her.

He blasted her. "The last couple of days? Lady, we've been treated like shit and kept in the dark since we dropped back onto this gone-to-shit planet. Don't tell us to be cool. We are way beyond that. Just tell us what you plan to do with us next so we can at least brace ourselves."

She said she was sorry, but she couldn't do that. And, at that point, there was no containing the fury that had been building. All of us, even the most measured and mellow, shouted at her with justifiable outrage. She was clearly out of her depth and just stood there, dumbstruck, waiting for someone to help her regain control. I figured it was up to me to rein in my crew—until someone told me otherwise, I was still their leader, so, yeah, my crew. Anyway, I shouted for everyone to settle down and let the woman speak.

Lucas chimed in, pointing out that she had the floor and hadn't been saying anything. I told Lucas to check himself and try to give the floor back to her. But I agreed with him. Sometimes I really hate having to be a company woman.

She stammered through what was probably the first piece of truth we'd been offered, explaining the situation was still in flux and they didn't know what was next. She said there were global considerations now that they had to sort through, and until they did, they couldn't make any moves.

Global considerations?! That sent us all reeling. Why were we targets of espionage and clandestine military operations? Surely, our little cosmic adventure wasn't that big a deal. We didn't even have any data that could make a difference. Not that they had a space program to do anything with it anyway.

She explained . . . actually just confirmed what we already knew . . . that we were taken by two collaborating governments—Russians and Africans. Our government did not know what their intentions were, but they believed it was in part to take advantage of the resources we were bringing back with us.

More confusion and ambiguity. Or as Hunter put it, diplomatic double-speak. They destroyed our ship. We had no resources.

And then a lightbulb seemed to go on for Hunter as he snarled at her, "Oh, you have got to be fucking kidding me!"

Abe asked him what he was talking about.

He snapped back, "Abe, you're a scientist . . . a physician. What do you think I'm talking about?"

Abe seemed as clueless as the rest of us until Hunter asked what resources they, as men, might have. A clue started to creep through the room if the looks on their faces were any indication. The spokeswoman registered the appropriate level of discomfort as she realized there was no containing this now.

I finally said to Hunter that if I was reading between the lines correctly, I thought he was saying he believed this government . . . OUR government . . . planned to use them to repopulate the planet.

He nodded and referred to it as forcing them onto a stud farm. It is unfathomable. What about civil rights? What about personal autonomy? What about . . . common decency? I mean, I know other countries have a history of this sort of abuse of power. Okay, so do we. A really ugly history. But I thought we'd evolved past that, had laws in place to protect against it. No wonder they are afraid of the shit storm. This is going to get ugly.

I was dumbstruck trying to understand how we didn't figure this out before now. I mean, we are all smart people! How had we not put two and two together? I asked Hunter how we could have missed something like this. He said he wasn't even thinking in that direction because it hadn't occurred to him that we weren't all affected too. After all, we had the biofuel on our ship. The difference was that we didn't ingest it, and they didn't bother to clarify that with us. They hadn't disclosed any of what they'd found in studying us like lab rats. I can't help but wonder if they intentionally kept us in the dark on that so we wouldn't come to this (now obviously) logical conclusion.

The avalanche of awareness crashed down on all of us, and no one was remotely capable of coping with it. Seeing as there was no getting us back in line, we were dismissed to get some food and rest. There were still so many questions, but I think everyone was kind of afraid of the answers. No one felt like eating, so we all just returned to our quarters to attempt sleeping.

We are supposed to reconvene in the morning. God only knows what tomorrow will hold. As I write that, I think of how, in the past, I've so loosely thrown that phrase around—"God only knows . . ."—and this is the first time it has ever felt like I mean it.

# CHAPTER TWELVE
## THE ACCOUNTING

Press Aide: Okay, when she comes in, you will have forty-five minutes, not a minute more. And please stick to the script. You got the list of approved questions, right? Good. Don't even try venturing off of that.

*[The aide goes to open the door and signals to someone on the other side of it without even waiting for a response.]*

Press Aide: Madam President, you'll sit here, and I will be off to your left in case you need anything. I will keep track of the time. We are on a tight schedule and can't go over the allotted time.

*[The aide retreats to a corner and President Marshall takes her seat. The remainder of the interview is on the record.]*

*Thank you, Madam President, for allowing me this time to talk with you. Your perspective on this is vital.*

Margaret Marshall (MM): Glad to do it. Where would you like to start?

*Wherever you feel the need to start. I understand you heard about this project and want to clear the record on some things?*

MM: Yes. First I want to say that our hearts go out to every member of the crew and their friends and family. This is an unimaginable situation and everyone is simply doing the best they can to make the right decisions for the good of an entire planet.

*Understood. You have come under a lot of criticism over how the crew has been treated, but I want to start by asking you about Major Lydia Statham. From what I understand, she had an impossible job dumped in her lap and was left to deal with many things above her pay grade, essentially being left holding the bag by her superiors.*

MM: That was unfortunate, yet unavoidable. My intention was never to throw anyone to the wolves. General Dunne had lined up Major Statham, one of our top administrators, to carry on with the team so I could return to DC to meet with the cabinet. She had a challenging task ahead of her, but we knew she could handle it. I could have let someone else handle everything, but I flew out there to meet with them to lay down the really hard news myself. And I am taking the heat for choices I did not make alone. But that is what leaders do. This is a classic no-win situation. Besides, I have never wanted to be the kind of president that hides from the hard parts. That's why I am sitting down with you today.

*And it is appreciated, ma'am. We will circle back to that; but, for now, tell us what happened in your meeting with the cabinet.*

MM: I was counting on the collective wisdom waiting for me back in DC to be sure. Hindsight suggests it may not have been the best choice to keep the presence of the crew a secret, but in those early days we were making minute-by-minute decisions and I was just trying to avoid making things worse.

*Worse how?*

MM: Well, we believed . . . and later had confirmed . . . that releasing them to roam free could set off an avalanche of unpredictable responses—from their remaining family and friends, from the public at large. The implications were huge and nearly catastrophic.

*That seems rather prophetic given what happened.*

MM: It doesn't take a genius to read some of the writing on the wall. We knew what it could mean, just not how the global reaction would escalate so quickly.

*I know the joint press briefing on the abduction was a unifying gesture, but what would you like to say about the role the Americas played in this?*

MM: Well, I can tell you they don't prepare you for moments like this. There really is *no* preparing for moments like this. And none of it is easy when you are making choices that affect billions of lives . . . and truly were made in the best interests of everyone. "Heavy is the head that wears the crown," as they say. Still, for the sake of global relationships, I had to try to justify my decisions to the other world leaders that were made without their input. They arguably should have at least been consulted, but there were many factors in consideration. I met with them to explain that. You know, there is a fine line between being antagonistic and standing your ground, and not everyone in politics knows how to walk it. This part of diplomacy is not fun. If I defended our position too firmly, I was an inflexible bitch.

*That's one word for it.*

MM: It's probably not the most presidential language, but . . . anyway, on the other side, if I apologized to keep the peace, I would be giving ground that could weaken us. And that was without even letting the personal loss of our soldiers get to me. All I really wanted to do was tear into Katarina and Lindi.

*That would be Presidents Katarina Petrova of the EEU and Lindiwe Adobwale of Africa.*

MM: Yes. They were the ones to initiate that . . . reckless and foolish op. But attacking your opponent . . . that's not what world leaders do.

Certainly not in *this* era. So we went in open to finding compromise. As you know, we held a summit in order to investigate and discuss the extremely unusual circumstances that had been unfolding so quickly. Everyone had questions regarding the recent turn of events and how they would be affected individually, as well as the impact on the world as a whole. The first to speak up was Priyanka Dewan, Prime Minister of the WEU. I think she was imagining saying to me many of the things I held back from saying to Kat and Lindi.

*So she accused you of being . . . What was it? Reckless?*

MM: And then some. She said, "With all due respect" . . . Let me tell you, as a person of influence, you hear that phrase a lot, and it rarely is accompanied with much respect at all . . . Anyway, she said, "You and your region have behaved unconscionably and you need to explain yourselves. The time for diplomacy has passed." That was no joke. She definitely wasn't using a diplomatic approach with me. She said "your," referencing the Americas, but it more often felt like an indictment on *me* personally. She felt our actions, and those of the EEU and African nations, presented a significant threat to the peace we have enjoyed for two decades, and she wasn't wrong. Speaking for everyone in the WEU, Asian, and Oceania regions, she said they were appalled and alarmed by the secrecy and duplicity of the last several days. I must give her credit. She is a strong leader; but, with the exception of Oceania, her region has the smallest territory and, therefore, least skin in this game. Still, I understood her concern, but I thought it was important to bring them up to speed on what we knew and where things stood at that time.

*You have the crew back on American soil now, correct?*

MM: They are in a secure location, where their needs are being met and their interests are being carefully guarded.

*Why all the secrecy? The whole world knows they are here now.*

MM: Yes, that is precisely why. The Africans and the Russians, in particular, have demonstrated they cannot be trusted. Their recent actions put those people at great risk and resulted in the loss of not only soldiers, but also one of the crew that was vital to the potential salvation of our planet. Of course they felt the same way about us. Katarina Petrova, in particular, was harsh in her criticism. She may be progressive, but there are still some obvious remnants of Cold War indoctrination in her. There was no delicate or diplomatic way to do this, and I was treading on thin ice. We were just trying to sidestep the potential this situation had for igniting conflict like we haven't seen in my lifetime.

*Do you really think it will come to that?*

MM: I am hopeful that can be averted after what we resolved in the summit. And, really, we are holding all of the cards. I made the decisions I did because I believe we are the best equipped to use this opportunity to everyone's advantage.

*That sounds rather arrogant, Madam President, with all due . . . Um, I mean, who are we to say we know best for everyone?*

MM: Honestly, I'm a bit disinclined to explain myself to you or anyone else. These other regions have no problem calling on us for help when they're in dire straits, expecting us to bail them out of their mishandling of resources. And they question our judgment now? And you don't have all of the information I do. The reality is the ship was ours. The crew was ours. It was our responsibility to assess the situation and handle it as we saw fit.

*But some of the other territories lent their own people to that crew. There were citizens of other nations on that mission.*

MM: I am aware of that, but the majority of them were Americans and it was a NASA-funded and NASA-initiated expedition. We had the greatest vested interest. Regardless, even if we had read them in from the beginning, none of them were, or are, in a position to deal with the consequences of the crew's return. These are all the same issues PM

Dewan raised and it was beginning to feel very territorial, which is not what we have been about since the pandemic. We have had to become a global community, and it has worked.

*Not without some hiccups though.*

MM: Of course not, but that's to be expected. But it was nothing like what the South Africans and the Russians have charged.

*What are their accusations?*

MM: Oh, they are dredging up ancient history. Well, not ancient, but going back to things that predate the pandemic, criticizing the Americans for loving to claim the moral high ground while annexing territory before the crisis and claiming the largest share of land and people since.

*That doesn't really make sense. The US hadn't been in the habit of colonizing for more than two centuries. What were they talking about?*

MM: They were referring to the purchase of Baja and the renting of other border zones in the mid-2020s, and the later acquisition of the remainder of Mexico. Also, that included the annexation of Cuba, which came around the same time, after sanctions and natural disasters crippled their economy. But that was under a very different administration and was not only financially beneficial to those struggling areas, but created an important buffer zone for immigration purposes. I don't have to tell you the crisis we were facing at the time. It is well documented in the annals of history. In fact, that happened before the *Alpha Centauri* team launched into space.

*They seem to be harboring the resentments of previous generations even though we don't operate that way any longer. But why are they holding that against us where the new territories are concerned?*

MM: As for what we acquired after the collapse, I don't know what unscrupulous actions they were imagining. The division of land and the remaining population was based on existing regions and voted on in a global summit, not a landgrab by power-hungry leaders. Their revisionist history definitely was not productive for what we were trying to accomplish, but they couldn't let it go. President Petrova suggested it was greatly to our benefit because our region has flourished, while the rest of them continue to struggle to survive.

*That is a fair assessment.*

MM: I know it does appear that way, though we are hardly flourishing. The standard of living in America has always been higher than that of Russia and the Eastern European block, and I recognize that their region was hit especially hard by the pandemic, but no part of this world was left unscathed. We had managed to work together for the last twenty years to contain this and retain some bit of hope for reversing the devastation. This was not the time to let petty resentments or disagreements unravel that unity—especially now, when we have been presented with a key to our salvation.

*What exactly are you proposing, Madam President? The rumblings that we have been getting are, quite frankly, disturbing.*

Aide: Okay, that's enough. President Marshall, let's go.

*[At this point the president and her entourage leave. I did not expect to get any further information on the summit, but I received an unexpected phone call that same evening. Following is the transcript of that call.]*

*Hello?*

*[silence]*

*Hello?*

LS: Hi . . . you know who this is?

*Yes. I am assuming you don't want to use your name though.*

LS: It would be safer if we didn't.

*I have to say, I've been really worried about you. I honestly did not expect to hear from you again.*

LS: I wasn't sure you would.

*What changed? Are you safe?*

LS: As safe as I can be . . . for now. I came into the possession of some information you need. It's too important not to take this risk.

*Okay. Is it okay if I record this call?*

LS: [silence]

*Hello?*

LS: I guess I have to trust someone, and you'd better get all the details straight.

*Okay. I'm recording. Just start when you're ready.*

LS: I know you talked with President Marshall today and you were cut short.

*How do you know that?*

LS: I can't tell you. Just trust me that it's from a reliable source.

*Okay.*

LS: So you were cut off when you asked about how they are planning to use the crew.

*Right.*

LS: And she was about to feed you some line about how no one likes the idea of what is often called for in times of war, and this was definitely a war. She was going to tell you we are facing a very different kind of battle—one for the survival of the human race. That is going to be the typical government spin for the nasty human rights violations they are planning.

*So you know what they have in mind.*

LS: Everyone at that summit knew. Only Malia Tauru from Oceania spoke up in opposition. They are really serious about human rights down there, but they don't have a lot of clout—no leverage—so they are treated like a nuisance, not taken seriously. Still, it's going to be hard for them to keep a lid on it, if the activists find out. That's why I'm calling you. I need you to call whoever you know. Get people mobilized.

*I got a quote Tauru gave a reporter shortly after the summit. She said . . . Hold on, let me find it . . . Um, yeah, she said: "We have never found the things done under the guise of the 'greater good' to be as necessary as asserted, and I do not believe this will be any different."*

LS: That's what they are afraid of. President Marshall will tell you that the "greater good" is absolutely reason enough to try whatever they can. The reason they convened the committee was to figure out how to avoid blowback, not to decide what to do. They had already decided that. They say they want to minimize the inconvenience to the crew, but that won't last long if that gets in the way of getting what they want.

*So let's back up. What are they planning to do with them?*

LS: To be clear, most of the summit was just for show, to placate the other world leaders who have already thrown colossally stupid temper tantrums over not being included. But Marshall knew she had to bring them into the fold to avoid any further disasters. So she road them in on what they found out in all the tests we ran on them when they arrived. We got valuable information. Actually—and this isn't where you need to focus your attention—we learned things that could lead to a cure.

*Wait. What? There's a cure?!*

LS: What did I just say? That is not the most salient detail.

*It's pretty damned* salient *to me!*

LS: Slow your roll. That could be years off. The more pressing issue is what they are planning to do in the meantime.

*Okay. What is that?*

LS: Well, they have seventeen men in their custody with viable genetic material that can be used to inseminate women who stand the greatest chance of carrying a pregnancy to term.

*Isn't that a massive affront to body autonomy?*

LS: Exactly! That's what I'm getting at.

*How do they think they can get away with that?*

LS: Sadly, there are legal precedents. But first they are planning to play on their honor, appeal to the sense of duty to serve humanity that led them to go into space in the first place. So effing manipulative! She called it another opportunity for them to be heroes.

*How do you know she said that?*

LS: I told you not to worry about that. Let's just say it was from a fly on the wall. Anyway, Petrova . . . the Russian president . . . wanted to begin collecting immediately and compiling a list of well-suited candidates. She said it was only fair that since their region suffered the greatest losses that they be first in line for the donations. That led to South Africa arguing that they should be first because they were nearly wiped out. She let it slip that when they went to Petrova with the intel they had about the return of the crew, they agreed they would share equally. Basically, they admitted they were planning to undercut everybody else.

*So, when Russia and South Africa abducted them, they were planning to keep them for themselves.*

LS: Was there ever any doubt about that?

*No, I suppose not. But weren't we going to do the same thing?*

LS: Of course. President Marshall will tell you we wanted to protect them and discover how we could use what they had to offer for an entire planet, not just our country. From what I heard, it almost turned into a catfight. It was like . . . instead of a landgrab, a *man*grab, and that isn't a good look on any woman.

*Okay. So I'm still trying to wrap my head around this whole proposition, but I have a question. What about the ratio?*

LS: What ratio?

*The race makeup. There are a lot of people with very different races who want in on this action. How is that going to work?*

LS: Good point. I haven't heard if they have considered that part—although I wouldn't put it past them to have calculated all of that already and put some kind of plan together.

*It's definitely cause for concern. The diversity of ethnicities on this planet has been severely compromised, and certain ethnic groups were hit harder because they were exposed longer and were already minorities.*

*I think it definitely has to be considered, but I'm disturbed by how that might play out.*

LS: I agree. To answer your question, after losing Harris in the retrieval, there are seventeen men remaining, eight of them are Caucasian, with varying heritage, but primarily European descent. Two are from the Middle East, three are of African heritage, two are Latino, and two are Asian. Across the whole group we found that two of the men are above the ideal age for producing a reliable percentage of viable sperm. These men may or may not be used, though they still have enough to be useful to them. And one of the young guys is sterile.

*I guess you learned all of this through the testing at Miramar. Did you take any reports with you when you left?*

LS: Didn't have time. I had to make a hasty exit. But I have a photographic memory, so I scanned as much as I could before I had to bail.
*I'm going to want to pick your brain for more on that later.*

LS: I hope there will be a later.

*I hope so too. For now, though, let's go back to what was covered in the summit. How are they planning to . . . um . . . distribute them?*

LS: Well, even they recognize it isn't realistic or reasonable to overuse the men who are minorities to keep the races "pure." There will have to be some . . . um . . . concessions. I'm guessing they will allow some personal choice in this. But there's bound to be more issues over the white people controlling all of this and deciding who comes out on top. Adobwale started down that road in the meeting, but Marshall shut it down pretty quickly so they could move forward.

*What did the other leaders in the room say? Were they okay with this plan?*

LS: PM Dewan asked Marshall to commit to full disclosure and full access to the crew. The Africans and the EEU both were on board, though that wasn't exactly a surprise. They have no choice but to cooperate. They need this too much. Tauru, however, said she had grave concerns for how this would manifest and promised she would not keep them to herself, if asked—hence the quote you got. She did, however, agree to hold back on any real judgment or public condemnation until she knew more of how the plan would be executed. I guess she considers what she said as stopping just short of public condemnation.

*There is one person you haven't mentioned yet, President Mai Hong of the Asian region. She was present at the summit, correct?*

LS: Yeah, she was conspicuously silent the whole time. Marshall finally had to ask her for her thoughts. She said because of China's history regarding population control, she found herself looking at our world facing the opposite scenario and she had concerns.

*Did she have any specific takeaway from her region's history?*

LS: She did. She had one recommendation she thought would ease everyone's mind. She suggested the crew be placed in a neutral zone—a region where no one would be regulated by jurisdictional constraints—and each of them would have an equal number of representatives on a governing panel to shape the policies for use going forward. Do you get that? *For use . . . not* for their protection, for their well-being, for their recovery and reintegration . . . for their *use*! This is why I need you to get activists pissed off and active.

*Okay, okay. I will start making calls as soon as we are done. What else did she say?*

LS: Alright, just don't screw this up. There is no time to waste. They agreed that no decision would be made unilaterally, and no decision would be executed without unanimous consent. At least it wasn't one crazy person calling all the shots. Maybe their crazy will neutralize each other somehow . . . or at least they will be too busy fighting over how to do this that it won't get done.

*Do they already have a location in mind?*
LS: The island that was New Zealand. They agreed it was the most viable option because of its location—I guess they figure a tropical paradise will make this more enticing—and its neutrality. It is also more isolated and easier to keep secure.

*So, when are they putting this plan into motion?*

LS: We have a little time. They still have several decisions to make and have to assemble a commission to make them, before they can actually fire up the assembly line. But the crew is being relocated to the new site as we speak.

*No wonder she was being so cagey when I asked if we had them back on American soil. Is there anything else?*

LS: Not now. I have to go underground again. You probably won't hear from me anymore, unless things change . . . Who am I kidding? Things are in a constant state of flux. If I learn anything else, I will figure out a way to get to you, but I don't know if I will have access to another phone anytime soon. Remember, you promised to get the word out. You can't wait until you release the documentary. This has to go public *now.*

*I promise. I promise. And I think I have exactly the perfect person in mind for this.*

# CHAPTER THIRTEEN
## BADGE OF HONOR

*How are you doing now, Amelia?*

AC: Oh, just peachy. Hey, by the way, thanks for the bail. My mom was trying to scrape together the money, but I am happy to get sprung early . . . and on someone else's dime.

*Happy to help. And thanks for giving me a little more time. Do you need anything before we get started?*

AC: No, I think I'm good. It's not like I did hard time. I suppose I should have been afraid, worried, anxious, or something other than annoyed, but I didn't have to worry about how my family would react. This was like a rite of passage. I'm getting a badge of honor, as far as they're concerned. And, let's be real, it's not like I suffered anything more than some minor inconvenience. I wasn't sent up the river for a nickel.

*You have such an unusual way of speaking for someone your age.*

AC: Yeah, well, I used to watch a lot of old movies with my grandma, who kept me when my mom was at work. And by *old*, I mean like *really* old, like from *before* this millennium old!

*Funny. That wouldn't seem so old to the crew, would it? Well, what happened when you were picked up at the rally?*

AC: Well, I think you have to call it a *protest*, not a rally, but that's probably neither here nor there. But we were making a bit more noise than some influential people liked, and they called in a "Disturbing the Peace" complaint. I guess I was really disturbing, because I got hauled in and booked. It was all pretty simple. Not like on TV. Although the officer sitting across from me looked rather disappointed that I wasn't quaking in my boots or shedding even a single, solitary tear. I kinda think she lived for that stuff. Made her feel powerful and superior. But I wasn't giving, and her face contorted into a scowl showing just how much she didn't like me . . . or herself . . . or the world, and then barked at me with an unnecessary amount of impatience. "Name?" To be honest, I couldn't help being a little contrary when I answered, "Amelia . . . Amelia Corcoran. *C-O-R-C* . . ." She snapped at me, "I got it, I got it. Age?" I told her, "Twenty-five . . . on my next birthday." I really wasn't sure why we were doing this. Big Brother knows exactly who all of us are and what we had for breakfast. They want us to think they don't monitor our every breath, but since the pandemic, no one does anything without it being tracked. And, really, the thing that bugs me the most is the farce of it all. Okay, that's not true. I'm still way more offended by the surveillance and the intrusion into all areas of our lives, but I guess it's adding insult to injury when they try to pretend they aren't doing it, or that it's for some noble purpose.

*So you don't trust the government either. Have you met Commander Young yet?*

AC: Who?

*From the crew.*

AC: Oh, no. I haven't had a chance to meet any of them yet. They kept me around to talk to the one guy, but I never actually even laid eyes on any of them.

*Maybe someday you will. Back to the police station . . .*

AC: Oh, yeah. So I must have spaced out for a minute, because she's yelling at me, "Miss? I asked for your address!" I do have a tendency for letting my mind roam off to other places I'd rather be when I'm stuck in an unpleasant situation. I couldn't help but wonder if she thinks about anything other than what the computer tells her to think about. So I started answering, and then I said, "Look, don't you have all of this on my license? You took that when you hauled me in here." She says, "Miss, we need you to cooperate so this can move quickly." Who wasn't cooperating?! I was just pointing out that it seemed to be a redundancy when she had all of my information accessible by looking up my ID, which she already had in her possession.

Then she says, "Miss, please just answer the question. Don't make this harder on yourself than it has to be." Boy, was I getting testy now. I said (not too calmly or quietly), "I'm not trying to make things harder! I'm trying to make them easier . . . for *everyone*! Don't you see that?" That's when she yells to some Amazonian across the room, "Halloran! We have a know-it-all over here who is refusing to give us her info. Take her down to holding and let's see if a few hours in a cell will loosen her up." She just had to announce that to the whole room as loudly as possible. And how does it make sense that being confined would loosen me up? I was right. She definitely let the computer do the thinking for her.

*Did that worry you?*

AC: Nah. I knew I'd be fine. Although Halloran, who was extremely burly and seemed to enjoy that aspect of herself, grabbed me by the arm, and the rest of me just kind of went with it, since my hands were still handcuffed behind me. I could tell she had a good six inches on me and probably eighty pounds, but even with that, I felt like she put extra effort into tossing me around like a rag doll. As she "led" me down the corridor to the holding cell, I passed multiple gawking faces attached to women of all ages. They'd been rounded up with me and were waiting for their turn to be called in for processing. Now they were suddenly stricken with fear that the manhandling I was subjected to was going to be their fate as well.

*They weren't as "experienced" as you?*

AC: Either that, or just not as dumb. I've had a few teachers and bosses tell me my blasé attitude is going to get me in trouble I can't get out of at some point . . . but not today. Once we rounded a corner and were out of sight, Halloran loosened her grip and slowed her pace. She smirked when I looked up at her, acknowledging she was making an example of me to scare everyone else into submission. I have to tell you, as if being jerked around wasn't bad enough, knowing it was all to intimidate other women, who were probably already scared out of their minds, really riled me up. Now that I'm out of this entanglement, I plan on organizing another protest over how we were treated. An activist's work is never done. And thanks for the tip, by the way.

*So this experience didn't change your mind any about "speaking truth to power"?*

AC: Not a chance! In fact, if they were hoping to shut me up, all they did was send me in search of a megaphone. I did get a little satisfaction in the moment though. Once we got to the holding cell, Halloran jerks on the large metal door and it doesn't budge. Apparently, the guard pressing the button to release it was a beat behind her. So she yanks on it again, this time with the force of embarrassment and frustration behind it, and it ricochets off the wall, nearly slamming into both of us. I promise you, it was everything I could do not to laugh out loud. But I knew if I hadn't restrained myself, she would have figured out a reason to put me in solitary.

*That must have been pretty gratifying.*

AC: It was, but it was short-lived. She shoved me across the threshold and slid the barrier between us with pleasure . . . *but*, also, with a great deal more caution. She glared at me for a long minute, attempting to intimidate someone. I figured she knew it wasn't working on me, but someone watching might get the shivers and be less of a hassle for her.

*Do you think that worked?*

AC: Eh, probably on someone. I was bored with the spectacle by then, so I turned and looked for a spot on one of those cold metal benches, where I could camp out until I got kicked from there. I didn't bother to see if Halloran had any parting gestures for me, but from the looks on the faces of the other women in the room, she did. As I scanned the available seating, an older woman—maybe in her mid- to late-sixties—scooted to the left a bit and pat the bench next to her. She had a nice face and looked clean and healthy, so I figured it was safe. I sat next to her and noticed she had the very distinctive scent of sandalwood and gardenias. It's an old-lady hippie sort of combo, just like my grandma wore. I knew pretty quickly I was going to like her. She was smiling at me and not in a creepy way, so I said, "Hi, I'm Amelia. What are you in for?" She laughed at my cheesy line, and I knew we were going to be friends.

*Yeah, that is pretty lame. Still, I get it; it's something I've always wanted to say too.*

AC: She said, "Don't you worry about it, honey. I thought it was cute." Doesn't that sound just like a grandma? She also told me it was refreshing to see someone my age who didn't have a perpetual deer-in-the-headlights look on their face. I guess a lot of my peers have only the one expression. To be fair, though, this world really has gone to hell in a handbasket on a level no one has ever seen. But the other thing is, this may have been my first time in the pokey, but it was not my first rodeo, if you know what I mean. Oh, yeah. She also thought I had an unusual way of speaking. I guess I do, for my generation. She laughed and it really reminded me a lot of Grams.

*Has your grandmother passed on?*

AC: No, I just mean . . . never mind. Anyway, I told her how I got busted at a rally for making too much noise and running my mouth to the wrong people. She was concerned about how my parents would feel about that. I told her, my mom will be so proud. Seriously . . . she is going to be over-the-moon proud. Like I said, I have a rich heritage of activists. I'm actually a little behind in taking on the family mantle. Grams says that the first time my mom got cuffs slapped on her, she was still so young and skinny that they slid right off her wrists. I don't know if that's true or not. Seems to me, they could have tightened them enough to restrain her, but it makes for a good story. The point being, she was protesting before she was in high school, so I'm considered a late bloomer. So this lady, she just sat quietly and listened as I rambled, and then it dawned on me that I was the one doing all of the talking, and I didn't know anything about her. Not even her name! I'm not sure if I wasn't getting any information from her because I hadn't shut up, or if she just wasn't divulging any. So I stopped, took a breath (which I don't think I'd done since I sat down), and said, "So, now that you know all about me, what's your name, and why are you here?" She said, "My name is Audrey, and I'm here for the same reason you are."

*So she was at the protest too?!*

AC: Sure was. I can't believe I didn't notice her. She was probably the only person even close to her age that I had seen at the station, either in the waiting area or in the cell. She was already in the cell when I got there, so I wasn't sure how she got there before me. She said she definitely noticed me. Said I was full of fire, and put up quite a fight. She said that I reminded her of herself when she was my age. That sounds about right. I wasn't done talking, I guess. That tends to get me into hot water a lot. But I'm used to it. It's just everyone around me isn't so much.

*I can definitely appreciate a talker.*

AC: I'm sure that's true. Makes your job way easier. Anyway, she said she was still super passionate in her outrage. She just didn't have the pipes to shout over everyone or the stamina to stomp around and get in their faces anymore. I asked, what got her out today? Had she heard what's been leaking about the *Alpha Centauri* crew? She said she was well aware, and couldn't sit at home and remain silent. Admittedly, it doesn't take much to get me to climb up on my soapbox. Finding a kindred spirit always gets my blood pumping—nothing like an echo chamber to embolden you in speechifying—so I was off again. I started ranting about how I just can't stand what they are doing to them! I mean, I'd be out here regardless, because this is the kind of injustice that just gets my hackles up anyway. But I feel I have a vested interest in this particular issue and I cannot sit silently by and watch this happen!

*Wow. You are still worked up, aren't you?*

AC: Oh, I am just getting started. She asked me why I was so invested. Even in my outrage I have enough sense not to broadcast all of my business. So I took a deep breath, scooted closer, and leaned in to whisper, like we were having some sort of covert meet-up. That's when I told her that even though I really shouldn't be telling anyone this, I thought I could trust her.

*Wasn't that a big risk? You didn't even know her last name.*

AC: Probably, but my gut usually isn't wrong about this stuff. So I explained that I work at the Space Flight Operations Facility, up in Pasadena, and was monitoring for space debris when the *Alpha Centauri* returned. I told her how I talked them down the whole way and had to chat up this poor guy named Lucas . . . and that's when it hit me.

*What hit you?*

AC: I said, "Whoa! This is really weird. He kept calling me *Audrey*. How crazy is that?! Strange coincidences."

*That is a strange coincidence . . . unless . . .*

AC: Yep. When I lifted my head to look at her, I could see her face had blanched, and I realized then that I was not talking to just any Audrey.

*That is so incredible! What did you say to her?*

AC: I just stammered a bit and said, "You . . . Wow! Oh, hey. You're her, aren't you?"

*Incredible. How did she respond?*

AC: This was the sad part. She said, "Yes. I never dreamed he would have remembered me. It's been four decades!" I said, "Yeah, but it wasn't four decades for them." Then I had to go and tell her that he not only remembered her, but he was crushed when he learned I wasn't her.

*Oh, that is tough.*

AC: No kidding. I felt so bad for them both. She said she really had hoped to meet him someday. But she couldn't now. Not like this. Not after all this time. I just didn't even know what to say at that point. I think I said something like, "This must be a big shocker for you. It totally makes sense why you'd be out there marching with us."

*There's not much else you can say.*

AC: She told me she had been an activist for most of her life too. In fact, she figured if my grandma was from this area, it was very likely she was hip to hip with her on an occasion or two.

*Is your grandmother from the same area?*

AC: Yeah, our family goes back a few generations in Southern California, mostly the Valley, so the odds are probably really good on that. But I really wanted to change the subject at that point, and I also had even more reason to get on my soapbox now. I asked, what part of this was bugging her most? For me it's probably the violation of privacy and personal autonomy. I just can't stomach how they have kept them locked up all this time and didn't tell *anyone* they were here. The thing is, I was sworn to secrecy. Actually, I was forced into it because they kept me at the office for three days under surveillance, monitoring all of my movements and not allowing me to have any contact with the outside world. They were so afraid I might spill the beans. And, truth be told, I probably would have. How do you keep something like this a secret?! The world deserved to know, if only to have some good news for a change.

*What about her?*

AC: She didn't really say. She just told me, "Amelia, you are too pure-hearted and idealistic for your own good, I'm afraid. And I don't know how you managed to hold on to a government job as long as you did with your obvious penchant for rigorous honesty."

*Good point. How have you managed that?*

AC: Honestly, I have been amazed myself. I guess it's because there isn't a lot of competition for my job, and I haven't made too much noise until now. But I'm not really counting on having a job, once they learn about this. It's okay though. I have a feeling everything will be changing everywhere now.

*I am sure you are right about that. I'm afraid the worst is yet to come.*

AC: Audrey said the same thing. How much worse can it get?

*I'm not at liberty to disclose everything I've learned from the various interviews I've done . . . not yet. I told you everything I could, when I called. Just . . . the only other thing is that just because we know they exist now, it doesn't mean we are getting full disclosure . . . from anyone. I'm just telling you to stay hypervigilant in putting pressure, wherever you can, on anyone you can, to find out what they are doing with them. They aren't going to be released just because the world knows they are here. It's too risky and there is too much potential fallout.*

AC: Wait. What do you think is going to happen? I figured there is something big they aren't telling us, but I don't know how we will find out what it is. I told Audrey about them destroying the spacecraft. Did you know about that?

*I did.*

AC: She didn't, but she wasn't surprised. She figured that is something that wouldn't ever get out.

*Oh, it will eventually. Give it time.*

AC: So, why do you think they did that? Maybe they brought back some alien life-form?

*I doubt it. I think that was probably more to cover up the fact that they came back, period . . .*

AC: Yeah, Audrey didn't think my Martian stowaway theory held any water either. She said either a cover-up of their return, or maybe to destroy the last traces of the corn.

*What do you know about the corn?*

AC: That they had biofuel on their ship for the return trip that was made from that corn they started feeding everyone and that caused the pandemic. Audrey told me that fuel was the original purpose, and it was never meant to be fed to humans or animals. It was just supposed to make rocket fuel. Something they conveniently left out of the history books.

*Amelia, you're going to find there are a lot of things that aren't reflected accurately. That's a big part of why I am working on this project.*

AC: I am almost afraid to ask . . . but I'm too curious not to. What else did they *not* tell us about the pandemic?

*That is a much longer conversation than we have time for right now. I got Audrey out of jail too, and am supposed to meet her at her house for an interview. Don't get into too much trouble. I may not be around with bail money the next time.*

# CHAPTER FOURTEEN
## FULL DISCLOSURE

Audrey Logan (AL): I find myself struggling with knowing where to start.

*Well, Audrey, maybe you could just start by telling me a little about your conversation with Amelia. I just left her an hour ago and she is spoiling for another fight already. I don't think it was just my conversation with her. So, what did you discuss with her?*

AL: Truly, I am in awe of what a small world it is—even with a literally smaller world than when I was her age—that we would end up in the same jail. I'm also stricken with amazement over the fact that we were rounded up for protesting a lot of the same things that have been issues for a century or more. Sure, which side you're on may have shifted, but what's at the core of the outrage remains the same. Sadly, most of this generation have no clue about how we got here, and seem too shell-shocked to begin to discover what lessons they can learn from the mistakes my generation and others made.

*Amelia certainly seems to have had her eyes opened from her time with you. And she seemed to be a pretty savvy young woman already.*

AL: Oh, yes, she is. Remarkable young woman. I have high hopes for her. I guess the place I started with her was before *Alpha Centauri* even left for their intergalactic adventure.

*When they were developing the corn?*

AL: No, hon, way before then. We need to go back to the 1970s when *Roe v. Wade* was instituted.

*Really? Why then?*

AL: I assume you know that was the decision that made abortion legal, right?

*Of course, but what does that have to do with this?*

AL: Well, in many ways it was the genesis of the argument we were making in our protesting. It was a significant turning point in the fight for body autonomy. But it never stopped being a hotly contested issue, and plenty of elections were decided based on the position a candidate took on the reversal or reinforcement of it.

*But it wasn't fully overturned, correct?*

AL: No, not exactly. A number of states chipped away at it by restricting access through individual local laws passed and by defunding the public clinics that offered the procedure. It was a constant seesaw of legislation that kept it basically legal, but hard to get.

*That is quite different from the way things are now, isn't it?*

AL: Yes, we once had a government that valued states' rights over federal ones. We have had to adapt to a different way of operating with the consolidation of population centers and so much loss. We didn't officially change the structure—there was no revision to the Constitution or anything so formal—we just gradually let more and more decisions be made at the federal level because it was practical. But what really changed on the abortion issue was an addendum to *Roe v. Wade* that was passed after the pandemic. Well, I should clarify, after the Apollo Corn Pandemic. We had a different one that swept across the globe a few years before that, and it had its own lasting impact.

*Oh, yeah. That one was a flu or something, right? It destabilized everything for a while.*

AL: Oh, my dear, it knocked out one of the girders in our civilized society. It started with a bunch of terminology this generation hadn't heard that sent them into a panic—social distancing, self-quarantine, shelter in place—that began to collapse an economy that was very dependent on communal spending.

*I'm not sure I follow.*

AL: People used to go out to restaurants and bars for social interaction. There used to be sporting events that drew tens of thousands of fans. Live music events in small and large venues were a big part of people's lives. I know that all seems foreign to you, but there was a time when that was a very normal part of life.

*No, I'm old enough to be familiar with some of it. And we do still have some of that. It's just not a prevalent part of our society any longer.*

AL: Well, when this other virus spread, and everyone was encouraged to stay home to prevent the spread of it, all of those forms of entertainment had to stop. It was only supposed to be for a little while, so the contagion could be contained, but it stretched from a couple of weeks into months. Many of the businesses just could not recover from the lack of income. Even though they tried to offer ways to stay operational without direct contact, too much of the population was out of work for a long time and they couldn't afford to order food from restaurants or pay for online entertainment.

*That's normal for us.*

AL: True, but for them, it wasn't. It was devastating. The good news is the virus did pass, and eventually people tried to resume a normal life

It was just never quite the same. That's why when the Apollo corn was invented, the possibility of a new world brought so much hope. Hope was something that had been sorely lacking for a while at that point. The corn later came to represent recovery here as well. So many areas were still suffering, or struggling to get back on their feet, which is why the ban on GMOs was lifted and Apollo corn was fully embraced by everyone. It was a way to feed far greater numbers of people in need in a shorter time frame. It was a fraction of the cost of other food sources. It seemed like manna from heaven to a weary and worried world.

*And this is what you told Amelia? No wonder she was ready to start a riot.*

AL: As I related this history for Amelia and relived it, I was ready to start marching again too. I couldn't help but feel an eerie sense of familiarity, of déjà vu, as I considered how the return of the *Alpha Centauri* crew represents hope for a world that long forgot what that means. I fear we may fall victim to the same tendency to pin everything on the possibilities they represent and make some fatal mistakes again.

*Based on what I am learning through these interviews and from information that has found its way to me, I fear you are right.*

AL: That's why I am so wary of what I see happening with the crew. Our world leaders, and most of the population, see them as a gift dropped right in our laps from heaven—the answer to all of our prayers. But there was some pretty ironic symbolism wrapped up in the name of that corn and what it did to us.

Apollo? *What's so symbolic about that?*

AL: The full name was APOLLO-VI-24—*Apollo*, because they named a lot of NASA missions that, and it was a nod to the history of innovation in exploration. Then *VI*—the Roman numeral for six—because it was the sixth version of the formula that was viable. And *24*, because they finished their research and got a successful material in the year 2024.

*Sure. I know that much. President Marshall explained the thought process behind the name.*

AL: Okay, but let's look at it closer. President Marshall may not even be aware of just how multilayered this is. So, how many letters does *Apollo* have?

*Six.*

AL: And *VI* is what?

*Six.*

AL: And if you take *24*, and add together 2 and 4, what do you get?

*Six.*

AL: And . . . what does that give you?

*Three sixes?*

AL: Okay, I guess I'm going to have to give you a little help. I forget how much of our literary history has been lost to this generation. You know, we lost ancient texts in the battles over the corn as large territories were set on fire and burned out of control. And even though so much was preserved online, our limited access to the internet means not a lot of people are reading these things. Plus, those types of subjects aren't really covered in schools anymore, since the practical supersedes the creative today. It's all focused on survivalist skills, trades, and labor. Hmm, let's see, have you ever read the Bible or gone to church?

*Yes, a little when I was younger.*

AL: Well, in the Bible, *666* is the mark of the beast. In the Book of Revelation, the last book of the Bible, there is a story of a coming apocalypse that is initiated by an evil force.

*I'd say we already kind of have that.*

AL: Well, no, we had a major catastrophe, to be sure, but this one they are talking about is the end of the world. The evil force—the beast, the Devil, Satan, whatever you want to call it—is represented by the number *666*.

*Why?*

AL: Um, back then—as in a couple of millennia before the earliest memories you have— there were a lot of people who believed numbers were symbolic, and they placed a lot of meaning in them. The number *7*, actually *777*, represented God, so giving evil a *6* meant they were less than God. Make sense?

*Sure, if you are going to buy into any of it at all.*

AL: Okay, so the fact that the name they assigned to the corn ends up being *666* is pretty crazy, right? Considering the damage it did to the world? It's the Devil's corn!

*Wow! Hadn't thought about it that way, but, yes, that is . . . quite the metaphor.*

AL: Quite a few people caught on to that when it was initially rolled out, but by the point they saw the symbolism, it was already a done deal. But what most of them didn't pick up on, and in my opinion is an even more creepy omen, is something most people don't know. Apollo was known as the god of knowledge, the arts, medicine, and prophecy, but most don't realize he was also the god of disease, famine, and plague.

*You're kidding! And no one picked up on that?*

AL: They were scientists. They did well to be creative enough to name it something other than its chemical compound. But my point in all of this is that our predecessors didn't stop long enough to consider the impact of messing with genetic material that way. Call me crazy, but I think they had some pretty powerful warnings from some cosmic force that giving it to humans and animals as a food source was a bad idea. And I think we are headed down the same road now. I don't think we are learning from history here.

*Well, that's a lot to think about and add to the context of everything we are learning.*

AL: I laid this out for Amelia as well, but it might be a bit much for her to consider, as her primary focus is the injustice she sees in keeping them locked away and not letting them decide how to live their lives. And that is most definitely part of it, but there are larger issues here, which brings me back to the *Roe v. Wade* addendum.

*I was wondering how all of this tied together.*

AL: So, after the corn pandemic, they couldn't go so far as to outlaw abortion again, but what they did do was make it so hard to get the procedure that few even tried. A couple of things factored into that. The big one was that science had advanced significantly in the realm of artificial wombs. You've heard of those, right?

*Of course. Kind of like incubators, except really early in the development.*

AL: Yes, essentially, they could take a fertilized egg and grow it from that stage into a baby without being inside a mother's womb.

*Just remarkable.*

AL: It is, but we aren't really using it much anymore. I'm sure the science and technology are still available, but with so few pregnancies that require that kind of intervention, it really isn't necessary. It typically only comes into play if a woman can't sustain a pregnancy to term and the baby is viable. We do still try to preserve every life possible.

*As we should. Shouldn't we have been doing this aggressively prior to the pandemic?*

AL: Well, my concern is that if they have any plans for trying to repopulate the earth, they might use those artificial wombs as a backup system. And, good Lord, that just seems so immoral.

*Why? Wouldn't it be a great, fast solution?*

AL: Well, there are a lot of people who believe that there are unforeseen consequences to bringing a child into the world that did not grow in its mother's womb.

*Are you one of them?*

AL: Yes. I believe there is a bonding and nurturing component to human development that starts in utero and can't be ignored. That is left completely out of the equation with this method.

*Okay, I can see how that would be true. But isn't that still better than the alternative?*

AL: Depends on what alternative you're talking about.

*Abortion . . . killing fetuses when humanity is in crisis for survival.*

AL: I thought reporters weren't supposed to project their opinions. Aren't you supposed to be impartial?

*I'm not expressing my opinion . . . just trying to get to yours.*

AL: Well, the debate about ProLife and ProChoice that surrounded abortion laws certainly made that their central argument—that we must do everything to preserve life. And they aren't wrong.

*So, why did the other side object to that?*

AL: They didn't object to preserving life so much as they objected to the government making the choice for a woman about what she would do with her body.

*Ah! And that's where the body autonomy argument we have now got started.*

AL: Well, it didn't get started there, but that issue is where it really came front and center for the first time. The thing is, most people who were labeled as ProChoice felt that each individual should be allowed to assess their financial situation, their mental and physical health, their family relationships, and other factors that were unique to them to decide what was best for them and any potential child.

*And why did the ProLife people have a problem with that?*

AL: Because they felt any of those concerns could be overcome with outside help and a child's life could be saved in the process.

*That also seems reasonable. Why was that a problem?*

AL: Well, a lot of the outside help they were referring to was wrapped up in other government and social welfare programs that these same people didn't want to fund. Adoption was a great option for some children whose parents can't care for them, but many more stayed in government-run facilities or foster homes and never really had a stable environment. For the mothers who decided to keep their children, but were poor or unsupported by a spouse or family, they relied on government assistance, but a lot of people resented tax dollars going to support those programs. A lot of mothers who found themselves pregnant had drug addiction issues. Some had other mental health issues. Those women had additional concerns about how pregnancy would impact their bodies and the babies they were carrying. My point is, it was a complicated issue and there really wasn't a one-size-fits-all solution if you looked at it with compassion and understanding. It didn't help that the labels each side attached to the other made it a very touchy subject and got a lot of people really angry.

*This is a tough issue. It seems pretty clear that we need to make sure we preserve every potential life right now if we have any hope of restoring the populations. But the idea of anyone telling someone else what they can or can't do with their own body . . . we definitely have some powerful arguments from history to factor in here.*

AL: Yes, we do. And that is what brought both Amelia and myself to the front lines of the protest today.

*Are there other aspects of this concerning you?*

AL: Most certainly. But they are mostly based in gut feelings at this point.

*I sense your gut is something we should pay attention to.*

AL: Oh, you are sweet, but you may be giving me too much credit. I'm just an aging woman hoping to see a brighter day before mine runs out. I hope I am wrong about my fears.

*So you think there is more to the story than what the public is getting.*

AL: Yes. I think we can expect to see the landscape change dramatically in the coming days and weeks. I don't think anyone really has a clue how this is going to play out. Even those who are making plans can't possibly anticipate how it's really going to work.

*How do you mean?*

AL: Well, if they get the astronauts to agree to what I think is on the agenda, there are many logistical and legal questions to answer, and many of them may not even be predictable. They will arise as we see this unfold. We are wading into some very new territory, and there is no road map whatsoever.

*It sounds like you have a better read on the situation than a lot of the people I've talked to.*

AL: I don't know about that. I may just have a little different angle to see the lay of the land, since I'm not in the trenches, and I've been around the sun quite a few times more than many of the people involved.

*I think they would do well to consult with you.*

AL: I don't really see that happening, and don't really want to involve myself that deeply. I'm content to hold a few signs and do an interview or two. The decisions that have to be made around this are far beyond the burden I can carry.

*Well, I am grateful for your time. I know you've had a long day. And, for what it's worth, I do hope you get your chance to meet Martin Lucas.*

# CHAPTER FIFTEEN

## REALITY BITES

*Martin, I want to start by saying how sorry I am for what happened to you, and I appreciate your being willing to discuss it with us.*

ML: Yeah, at first I didn't want to, but it seems like something the public should know . . . or the leaders . . . or somebody outside of the center.

*Has the Marshall administration reached out to you yet?*

ML: Oh, sure. They were notified as soon as . . . Well, soon after it happened.

*Okay. Well, take your time, and we'll only do what is comfortable for you. But can you describe what went on that night and the next day?*

ML: Some of it is still fuzzy, but I remember lying in my bed thinking, "Two more hours. I can get through the next two hours." That didn't seem like such a big deal. I figured once the sun was up, people would be getting to their daily business, and I would have plenty of distractions. I just had to get through the next two more hours. All I had to do was *not* think for two more hours.

*What did you think would happen then?*

ML: I'm not really sure. I guess it was unrealistic to think I was going to shut my brain off at that point. But maybe I'd at least have someone to talk to then.

*You didn't want to wake anyone to talk?*

ML: No. I couldn't figure out what to say at that point. What was there to say?

*Well, I think you could just start by telling someone what you experienced. You talked to Hunter, didn't you?*

ML: Yeah, I did end up talking to him. I just couldn't bring myself to wake someone in the middle of the night for something like this.

*For* something like this*? I would think this is* precisely *the kind of thing you'd wake someone to report.*

ML: I mean, yeah, I guess. It's just not as easy for men . . . I mean, not that it's easy for women . . . That's not what I mean at all. I just mean that it's easier for women to talk about stuff, period. God, I think I'm digging myself into a hole here.

*Martin, it's okay. Just take a breath and regroup. There is no pressure. Continue when you're ready.*

ML: I'm okay. Let's just get this over with. The thing is, I know there's the stuff that happens in prison, but can a guy *really* get raped by a woman? Seriously. It's not like I wasn't horny as a . . . whatever . . . a frat boy? And who wouldn't be? It turns out I hadn't had sex in over forty years. But I didn't exactly picture breaking my dry spell that way. But is it really the same? It's not like she beat me up or held a knife to my throat. It wasn't violent. Damn it. What the hell is with these waterworks? Why am I crying over something like this? . . . Again. I had a meltdown with Hunter and Dr. Tilden too.

*This is a perfectly normal reaction.*

ML: But . . . this is the thing I struggle with . . . I have to be honest, parts of it felt good. Doesn't that make it consensual somehow? If part of me enjoyed it? Although some of the stuff she said to me didn't sit too well with me—especially when I woke up and tried to resist. I don't . . . I don't know what I'm feeling.

*What did Commander Young and Dr. Tilden say to you?*

ML: Oh, well, Hunter, he was like, "Jeez, Martin, what do you mean, can a guy get raped by a woman? Of course they can, and it doesn't have to be violent to be rape. How do you not get that? You were part of that supposedly 'woke' generation."

*He's right, you know.*

ML: I guess. Then Dr. Tilden tells him, "Hunter, go easy on the boy. He has suffered a trauma, and one that men are sorely equipped to process. We are conditioned to believe men are always in the mood for sex and won't ever turn it down, so the idea of being forced into it is inconceivable."

*You do a pretty good impression of both of them.*

ML: Thanks, I had plenty of time to practice on the mission. We had to entertain ourselves somehow. But, you know, what he said, that's what I've been asking myself. I mean, I wanted sex, but not like that. I don't really know how to explain what I am feeling. Did I somehow invite it unknowingly? . . . I mean, she said that I had to want it. It had been such a long time and I deserved to have some fun. She said, if I just relaxed, it would be over soon. Oh god! Is this how women feel? Oh god, oh god! What have we been doing to them?!"

*It's okay, Martin. Don't give yourself a panic attack. Easy. Easy. And, to answer your question, unfortunately, from what my female friends have told me, yes. And I am sorry you have gained any level of firsthand knowledge in this area.*

ML: My chest keeps tightening and there is a huge lump in my throat the size of a baseball. This happened earlier and Dr. Tilden told me to lean my head between my knees and he patted me on the back.

*Do you want to try that again?*

ML: No, to be honest, I really don't want to be touched right now. I didn't then either, but I didn't want to offend him.

*Don't you worry about it. Do what you need to do and let me know if you want to stop.*

*[At this point, Martin gets up and paces around the room for about ten minutes, then sits back down.]*

ML: Okay. I'm ready. Hunter told me to calm down too and gave me some tips to get a grip on myself. Then he asked me to try to run it back for them—to tell them from the beginning what I remembered.

*Do you feel up to doing that for us now?*

ML: Yeah, they say I need to get used to talking about it because it helps to process it. Plus, I have a feeling I'm going to be retelling it a lot for all the people who are going to get involved. So I was asleep in my bunk. Having a pretty decent dream, I might add . . . but not anything sexual. We were back on the ship, and I was bobbing and weaving around an asteroid field. It was some really impressive navigation, if I do say so myself.

*Sounds like you were in your happy place.*

ML: For sure. So I was alone in my bed, not awake.

*Okay.*

ML: I was telling all this to Hunter and then I realized I had been calling him by his first name, and all of a sudden I got really freaked out that I was being too informal with him for some reason, like this sort of situation called for using ranks and last names or something. I almost started calling him "sir." But he was like, "Look, Lucas, I think we can dispense with the formalities at this point. We aren't on the ship anymore and we are about as up close and personal as it gets here, so rank matters shit all about now." And, yeah, I guess that is pretty personal.

So I was asleep and dreaming, but then the dream stopped, or morphed into a half-dream, half-reality situation. I didn't feel awake, but I wasn't on the ship anymore. I was in my bunk and things seemed way more real, like I could feel the sheets on the bed. Then I started to sort of feel someone touching me. I was in a heavy mental fog, but didn't feel like I was actually asleep anymore. That's when I started to realize the part of me I felt someone touching . . . and I was getting . . . um, hard. Sorry. I don't know . . .

*It's fine. Go ahead.*

ML: I wasn't sure what was happening, but it did feel good. Then I felt a weight pressing down on me. I'm not sure if I had opened my eyes before then, but I did at that point and saw a dark figure. A woman. She was straddling me.

*Martin, I am so sorry. That must have been . . . It's not something anyone wants to imagine happening to them.*

ML: I really didn't know what to do. It was over before I could even think straight enough to try to make my body react. When I did, I realized I couldn't have moved my arms or legs if I'd wanted to. I was tied down. Even if I wasn't, she must have slipped me something, because even after she untied me, I couldn't move. Dr. Tilden said they would do a tox screen, but he figured it was a mild sedative.

*That sounds highly likely. Any thoughts on how she might have slipped it to you?*

ML: Not a clue. Probably won't ever figure that out, but Dr. Tilden guessed it wasn't much or I wouldn't have been able to . . . you know.

*Achieve an erection and ejaculate. Martin, it is okay to speak candidly. There is no judgment here, and these terms are not offensive.*

ML: Okay. It's still just a little awkward to say them to a stranger in this kind of setting. I can't even really talk about this stuff with my doctor.

*I understand. Again, we are not going to ask you to do any more than what is comfortable for you. No pressure.*

ML: Thanks. Oh, you know what was weird. I think she said "thank you" when she was cleaning me up.

*Really? What do you think she meant by that?*

ML: Well, apparently, she had put a condom on me. She was really careful about removing it too. It wasn't like it usually is where you just pull it off and get rid of it. In fact, I think she put it in some kind of bag.

*What in the world? Why would she have done that?*

ML: Hunter thinks she was saving it . . . *Harvesting* is what I think he called it.

*Oh, you can't be serious.*

ML: Hunter seems to be convinced that's what was going on. He said we already knew they were sequestering us here so they could decide how to use us. He told me he and Dr. Tilden had been having lots of conversations about our "potential."

*Your "potential"?*

ML: Apparently for repopulation. He thinks this chick . . . woman . . . took advantage of her access and jumped ahead of the line, so to speak. When he said that, I was like, "Whoa, whoa, whoa! Are you saying she stole my swimmers so she could get herself pregnant?" I really thought I was gonna be sick.

*Do you feel okay now? You are looking a little pale.*

ML: I don't know. Why do I feel like this? I can't seem to get a grip. I really do want to hurl. I also want to scream and cry. I want to throw things and hit things. What is wrong with me? I mean, a lot of the other guys were making fun of me for complaining . . . that I didn't get to bitch about having sex when they missed out. It was just sex, right?

*Absolutely not. It was about the furthest thing from sex. It was a violation.*

ML: Hunter said that too. I just can't get my brain around it. He called it an affront, an assault. He said you don't have to come away with cuts and bruises for it to be that.

*He's right. You didn't agree to it, did you?*

ML: No. I wasn't even awake to do that. I can't say for sure that I would have, had I been awake.

*And that's the whole point! Someone did something to you without your knowledge or consent. They took away your free will, your agency, Martin. And then, on top of that, they took away some of your genetic material. There is nothing about this that is normal or okay. You have nothing to be ashamed of or sorry for. And don't for a second think you could have done something to stop it. She drugged you. This was a crime, plain and simple. I hope those in charge of the facility will be pursuing this to bring her to justice.*

ML: It sounds like they will. But I'm not sure if it's about me or them, to be honest. I just don't even know what to do with this. After talking to Hunter and Dr. Tilden, I needed some time alone to think. Suddenly the daylight I was waiting for didn't feel so appealing any longer and I just wanted to be back in the dark, in my bunk . . . very much alone. I just got up without another word and walked out of their quarters and stumbled back to my own. Thankfully, I was able to get back to my space without making eye contact with anyone and was able to just curl up under the covers and fall asleep.

*I'm glad you were able to rest. I understand they did come and talk to you later . . . the director, I mean.*

ML: Yeah. She came in and woke me up a couple hours later. I guess it's to be expected that I would nearly come out of my skin from this hand on my foot and an unfamiliar voice calling my name. I really hope this isn't what I am going to have to live with for the rest of my life . . . this . . . PTSD response every time I wake up. I don't know if I can deal with that.

*Getting counseling will help with that . . . and time.*

ML: I guess we'll see. Anyway, her name is Dr. Sandra Pope. She was brought in to oversee the facility and she told me Hunter and Dr. Tilden went and talked to her about what happened to me that night. She said she needed to ask me some questions. I didn't really want to go through all of it again so soon. But she said we needed to so they could try to find out who did this. She said she would also be asking me to speak with our on-staff psychiatrist about it as well. She said how I process this incident was really important and they wanted me to have the right support. So I will be getting that therapy you mentioned.

*She's right. It will make a big difference in the short and long run.*

ML: She told me it's really not an option. They need me to be in tip-top shape mentally, physically, and emotionally. She said it was their priority.

*Now I see why you said you think it may not be entirely about you.*

ML: In addition to that, they went into a frenzy like their hair was on fire. They were securing everything and setting up new protocols for who has access to us and where we can go when. It certainly didn't feel like we were there voluntarily . . . not that we really thought that anyway, but we at least thought we could probably get out and about a little. We found out pretty quickly that was not the case.

*Did they tell you that you couldn't leave?*

ML: Oh, it was more than that. And I wasn't the only one who had trouble.

*You mean she assaulted someone else that night?*

ML: Not her . . . and not that night. One of the comms guys—Pearce . . .

*Pearce Johnson? Isn't he the one who figured out your communication with Ground Control had been cut before landing?*

ML: Yeah, that's him. And that's something we still haven't gotten an answer for, by the way. But he found out about what happened to me, and between that and the shady stuff about the comms he'd been sitting on, and everything else just piling up, he kind of snapped. They were already putting us in full lockdown, and he hacked the system long enough to make a break for it.

*Really? So he got out?*

ML: Only for a hot minute. He was running from the compound, which, by the way, is not as carefully guarded as you might expect because he got past the perimeter fencing pretty easily and was on his way to the main road when he ran right into a mob of women that was congregating around the facility trying to get a peek at us. He was nearly mauled within an inch of his life! I heard they saw him and yelled, "Fresh meat!" And then they pounced on him.

*Why would they do that?*

ML: I don't know. And they probably didn't actually say that. You know how these things get blown up. I don't think they meant to hurt him. Apparently, they were just so excited . . . Things got out of hand. Each of them just wanted to get ahold of him for herself. But they nearly pulled him apart until the guards pushed their way through to him. From what I heard, there must have been thirty or forty women. That could have been an exaggeration. Men do like to inflate numbers. But, regardless, it was scary as hell, and they used that to really drive home the point that we were much safer inside. No matter what they plan to do with us in here, I guess that's probably true. It's a jungle out there.

*That is really unfortunate. So, what happens now?*

ML: *Now?* I guess now I go back and become one of their lab rats . . . until I die . . . or run out of juice . . . pardon the pun.

*So the rumors are true. This is basically a government-sanctioned sperm bank.*

ML: Hunter keeps calling it a *stud farm.* Yeah, I think that's what's coming, though they haven't told us specifically yet what that's going to look like.

*This lone bad actor aside, is there any truth to the other rumors?*

ML: Like what? You know we don't have any contact with the outside world.

*You know what, don't worry about it. You've been through enough. No need to add to it all. Martin, hang in there. There is a lot of help available. You only have to ask for it.*

ML: You sound like . . . I don't know . . . like you've been where I am.

*Well, the pandemic . . . made a lot of people do a lot of desperate things. Just . . . just know you're not alone, and it will get better.*

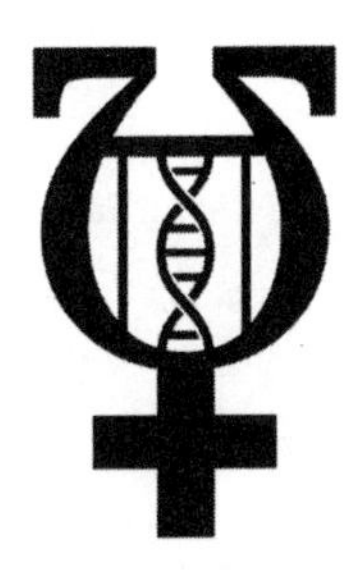

# CHAPTER SIXTEEN

## THE TRUTH FROM DOWN UNDER

*Dr. Tilden, thank you for the follow-up. How have things been since you left Kaikoura?*

AT: I guess the best way to put it is . . . challenging.

*Why is that? Isn't being free to live your life, and be with Sarah, what you'd been waiting for?*

AT: Oh, certainly. It just has not gone as we had hoped. I am not sure we knew what to expect, but leaving the facility has had its own drawbacks.

*Why don't we back up a bit and talk about how you got out in the first place?*

AT: Sure. So you know about the horrible attack on poor Lucas, correct?

*Yes. It got out quickly and became fodder for President Marshall's opponents. The uprising was swift and loud.*

AT: Yes, it certainly was. Well, those protests led to a serious accounting for the practices around our situation, and the world leaders convened to determine what had to change and how. They were not prepared to release us all, but it was becoming clear there had to be a better plan for the future.

*It sounds like a plan, period, was in order.*

AT: Quite true. There did not seem to be much of one, other than moving us to the center in Kaikoura, New Zealand.

*As far as detainment facilities go, a tropical paradise isn't all that shabby.*

AT: We certainly had been in far worse places. However, the uncertainty around how long and for what purpose we would be held was becoming increasingly troublesome for everyone . . . not just Hunter.

*So his suspicions were catching on with everyone?*

AT: How could they not? We had all seen and experienced far too much to believe we were being held for our own safety. And yet our safety was one of the primary reasons they gave for what they were doing. Then when poor Pearce was assaulted while trying to leave after Martin's attack, they used those circumstances to drive home the fear of danger lurking around every unsupervised corner.

*How did they convince you you'd be safer with them than outside, when what happened with Martin was an inside job?*

AT: That was part of the plan they presented to us. It detailed exactly what they were hoping to get from us and what they committed to providing in return. It was the most specific information we had been given since our return.

*Though they have not gone public, the details are leaking out. Can you go on record to confirm or correct what we're hearing?*

AT: We were required to sign a contract, but it did not include a nondisclosure clause. I am not sure if that was an oversight . . . though

I cannot imagine they would, even in their haste, overlook something so important if they thought it mattered. My guess is that their interests are better served by giving us room to breathe. In other words, not being muzzled or restrained any further.

*Okay, so what can you tell me about the deal?*

AT: First I should clarify that the deal was not presented as the proverbial offer you can't refuse. We were free to reject it, though they did make a hard sell for staying. This, of course, did not apply to the female members of the crew. They were simply given a settlement commensurate with forty years of back pay, adjusted for inflation, of course. They were promised any reintegration support necessary and the opportunity to settle wherever they chose, whether in their home countries or expatriation to another. They were also offered assistance in finding new career paths through continuing education or training—for free—or skills assessments for application in other fields.

*There has been a good bit of public outcry about this. Some see this as unfair considering there are hundreds of thousands of people who also have been left without jobs or places to live after the pandemic. What about them?*

AT: I have no insight on what happened during the time we were gone. But, for the women on our crew . . . it was through no fault of their own and in service of the greater good that they found themselves in this situation. Surely, you can see why such measures were appropriate.

*Yes, but most of the people affected by the pandemic didn't bring that on themselves either. I am not suggesting they don't deserve the help. I'm just pointing out that there could be major blowback, particularly in the Americas, over what some are calling a "sweetheart of a severance package."*

AT: I am not sure what to say to that other than I do not begrudge these women what they are getting, nor do I feel the compensation the men are receiving is unwarranted.

*Okay, let's get into that.*

AT: Well, for those who were willing, there was a two-year proposition to stay at the center and provide their genetic material for use in research and development of a cure for the damage done by the pandemic, as well as for use in repopulating the planet . . . with an option to extend their service if necessary.

*And what would they get in return?*

AT: In addition to the same package the women were given for their lost years, these men would be provided all necessities—shelter, food, medical care—and a monthly fee for their donations.

*How much was that?*

AT: If they maintain a schedule of providing samples two to three times per week, they will receive $1,500 per week. They will not receive the money until the end of their contract. If they terminate early, they will receive compensation, but at a prorated figure depending on how much of their contracted time they completed.

*That's a significant amount of money in this economy.*

AT: Fair, wouldn't you say, considering the service to humanity?

*Sure, I guess. Yet you opted out. Why is that? Did you have a problem with the whole thing?*

AT: Well, I was not an ideal candidate in the first place. I am in my sixties, and though I am in good health, it is not optimal. They would have used me, anyway, because they are playing a numbers game in this, but I chose not to be included for personal reasons as well. My wife and I never had children of our own. There may have been fertility factors in play there. We never checked. But we discussed it, and just felt if I were to produce any offspring, it would be with her as long as she was alive.

I could not, in good conscience, father a child with anyone else, having not made every effort to do so with her first.

*So, are the two of you trying?*

AT: No, that is not really the point. The odds of Sarah having a healthy pregnancy in her early fifties are significantly reduced, so we are not taking that risk. But I cannot cause her the pain of knowing another woman is bearing my child.

*You don't think that's a bit selfish?*

AT: Perhaps, but it is our prerogative to do so. We aren't alone.

*Who else opted out?*

AT: Kamil Awan, who also is beyond the ideal age, chose not to participate for religious reasons. We did have another young man—Sean Flemming—who was disqualified because they found he was sterile, due to a genetic abnormality from birth. He and his twin sister, Natalie, wanted to stay together anyway. They have done everything together since the beginning—joining the academy, applying for the mission, and then going on the journey—and with their parents gone, they only have each other. I do wish them well. They have a special bond and it should get them through.

*Everyone else was on board?*

AT: Most of the young men on the crew were lured in by the money, as well as the fact that they did not have lives to return to anyway. Of course sense of duty was a factor too. Honor and public service are obviously important to these fellows.

*I still can't believe Martin stayed . . . or went back . . . after what happened to him. You know I talked to him after the incident.*

AT: Yes. He is struggling. He chose to leave initially, which is the only reason you had access to him. But he found life on the outside more terrifying than he expected, and he is not at the place where he is ready to face his family. For him this feels like the safer route, and perhaps there is a little Stockholm syndrome going on. One could argue he is hiding from reality, but I suppose we all process our grief in our own ways. Staying put is the way for him. And maybe it is his way of facing the monster head-on. Who are we to judge?

*He is stronger than I would have been in those circumstances. So no one else was opposed to this plan?*

AT: Oh, Hunter considered not participating, but he decided that since he was getting older and had no children of his own, there was no reason not to do this for the greater good.

*A guy like Hunter? He could have a couple running around out there he doesn't know about.*

AT: Well, you could be right about that. If he did, they would have to be . . . let's see . . . about your age, I guess.

*Um . . . moving on. And speaking of those left behind . . . you all were finally allowed to check in with family and friends, correct?*

AT: Yes, once the word was out about us, our families, in particular, were clamoring to have contact with us. Once we were settled in New Zealand, we were allowed to have video calls with them.

*That must have been strange. I guess many of you have lost loved ones who were older when you left.*

AT: Some old, some not so old. The pandemic took a lot of our people through the warring and the related diseases. None of mine and Sarah's peers or siblings are still around. We have a few nieces and nephews, who are about our age now. That is a tough thing to comprehend for certain. The eerie thing is they look so much like their parents, it is almost as if we have them back. Many of the younger crew members still have their families alive, but forty years is a generation and a half worth, so parents are now the age of grandparents, siblings are now the age the parents were when these young people left.

*What about Kamil Awan? I learned through a letter from Captain Halverson that he and his wife were estranged when he left. Has he returned to his family?*

AT: Oh. No, his wife is gone. His daughters, who were young adolescents at the time, are adults with families of their own. He has been in contact with them and has plans to move close to his eldest daughter, but reentry into their lives is going to take time and patience. It will for all of us. And, speaking of Captain Halverson . . . what a tragedy. Sarah and I were beside ourselves.

*What happened? Her journals were sent to me anonymously and I have not been able to get any specifics about her death.*

AT: I imagine that is due to an overabundance of caution around concerns for liability.

*I must say, the tone in her journals seemed to be increasingly despondent. Did she . . . I hate to ask . . . but did she take her own life?*

AT: No, no. The change in her demeanor was likely due to everything she had been through, coupled with her deteriorating health. But she was nowhere near the point of suicide. Please be clear about that. I will not have her reputation tarnished . . . I am sorry. That is not to say such action is shameful. I am simply guarding against causing any of her loved ones undue pain.

*Understood. What was the cause of death?*

AT: You see, the head wound she sustained in the landing seemed to be a pretty straightforward concussion, with a fairly sizable scalp laceration.

It appeared to be nothing that would present any long-term problems. However, there was a clot that formed at the point of impact. Even that would have been manageable with close monitoring and a blood-thinner regimen. What we did not detect was a congenital abnormality that created a weakened arterial wall, and as the clot moved through, it strained the vessel to the point of rupture. She died in her sleep of an aneurism. There was nothing that could be done. So very unfortunate, and a great, great loss of a remarkable woman.

*Yes, it is. I wish I had had the opportunity to talk with her. Reading her writings revealed she was someone I would have liked to know. And every member of the crew speaks so highly of her. Getting back to the reintegration process, what have you heard from the others who left the compound?*

AT: I have not been in touch with most of the women on the crew since their departure. I would guess they are facing the same challenges Sarah and I have, and what Kamil has reported to me too. Finding many of those we knew to be gone or not at all how we remembered them has made getting our bearings quite difficult. We are trying, but it is almost easier to keep to ourselves. I must admit, there have been fleeting moments when I have thought we would have been better off to have remained in the compound with the rest of the crew. They really had become our family after all we had been through together.

*Has your wife felt the same?*

AT: We have not discussed it, though she has made comments in passing about missing her "children." I believe the crew members were her surrogates in many ways. I dare say they would like to have us back with them too. Given the opportunity, I think most of us would consider re-forming a community together, though maybe with fewer confinements and dictates.

*What kinds of dictates have they imposed?*

AT: Much of it is commonsense guidelines for ensuring optimal health—diet, exercise, sleep regimens that will keep the men in tip-top shape medically as they provide for the repopulation. Of course no alcohol or drugs, no sexual relationships, no leaving the facility. While those are reasonable under the circumstances, these young men have been through a lot. They were hoping to go out and have a little raucous fun when they got home.

*How much . . . I guess there's no polite way to ask this . . . how much are they expected to produce?*

AT: As I said earlier, the contract is for two to three samples per week. That is based on the fact that the ideal time frame for collection is no less than every two to three days, but no more than five to seven. Sperms need time to develop and grow, but the older they are, the more likely they are to have defects or motility issues, and they die relatively quickly. Did you know that at least 25 percent of the sperms in an ejaculation are dead? And it is likely that only 25 to 30 percent are going to be viable for reproductive purposes.

*No, I can't say I have delved that deeply into understanding my swimmers. So, how are they expecting this to turn around the population problem with only fourteen men contributing to the bank? Wouldn't that take decades?*

AT: Well, a single ejaculation typically has at least 40 million sperm. Even if only 30 percent of them are viable, that is still 12 million. Multiply that by fourteen men, three times a week, and you have quite a lot of material in the bank to work with. Conservatively . . . and theoretically, of course . . . one specimen could potentially fertilize 240 eggs. With steady production over the course of two years, they could produce as many as 1 million babies, and that does not even take into account the possibility of multiple births, which is not uncommon. And let us not overlook the fact that they will be vigorously studying our DNA to find a cure. There is real promise there for turning all of this around in such a way that we will not have to start from scratch, if you know what I mean.

*That does sound promising. Are there any potential problems there . . . aside from the unsavory nature of this whole idea in the first place?*

AT: I share your distaste for all of this, however I do not really see any way around it if we are going to save the human race. I do hold concerns for the increased odds of genetic abnormalities with such a shallow gene pool.

*What, like birth defects?*

AT: Yes. There is an exponentially greater likelihood for recessive genes to become dominant when there are so many shared markers. The logical answer for that is gene mapping and selection . . . However, if we have learned anything from the pandemic—at least I hope we have learned from the pandemic—that genetic modification is very tricky business and holds within it an unseen world of unpredictable outcomes. But there is at least the science available for removing defective sperm to increase the chances of a successful and healthy pregnancy. That should even out the odds some.

*That does sound promising. So, what's next for you and for the others?*

AT: That is a very good question, my friend. I imagine it will be a day-to-day process of figuring out where we fit in this new world, and what part we want to play. We have no jobs or homes to return to, so every decision includes a fresh start. That can be overwhelming, as it holds infinite possibilities, but it is quite thrilling as well. Things have changed so much all over the globe, but especially in our home country. Sarah and I may take some time to just travel and explore. Suss out the options before we land anywhere permanent. I do hear of some significant political unrest brewing back home. We may do well to avoid that for now.

*You mean the rumored split?*

AT: Yes. There have been rumors of such secessions of different states in the past—Texas, California . . . California and Oregon as the State of Jefferson . . . California, Oregon, and Washington as another Pacific Northwest territory—but none of them ever manifested for a number of very good reasons. I am not sure if those reasons still exist. Not knowing how our government is structured under the new aggregation, perhaps the constitutional obstacles are no longer there. I would imagine the economic considerations have changed as well. The balance of differing ideologies has been the bedrock of our democracy from the beginning, but this became a divide . . . a fissure . . . in our foundation in the years leading up to our departure. It seems that has reared its ugly head once again. I do not think there is enough unity to hold it together any longer. We shall see.

*It definitely seems we are headed that way. Dr. Tilden, I do appreciate your time. Please stay in touch and let us know where you land.*
AT: I certainly will. And you might want to have another conversation with Hunter when you are ready. He deserves to know.

*I . . . um . . . What are you talking about?*

AT: You are his son, are you not?

*What? How did you. . . ?*

AT: You have his eyes and that same fire in your belly.

*You won't say anything to him, will you?*

AT: No, son, that is yours to tell.

# CHAPTER SEVENTEEN
## A BRAVE NEW WORLD

*Hunter, I'm glad to finally catch up with you.*

HY: I'm sorry it has been so hard to connect. Since the White House fiasco, I had to go to ground. And I guess you know I've been with Statham, since she is the one who put you in contact with me.

*Yeah, so tell me about that.*

HY: Okay. As you know, Statham was confronted by a guard after our closet meeting and she, rightly, assumed there would be no way to keep a lid on that. So, before they could take action, she put her training to good use and went off grid. Fortunately, she had a few connections—people who did not support the actions of the administration and were in a position to keep her hidden and safe.

*I had really worried about her after our first contact. She disappeared without a trace, and every source I had—and I have a few with a pretty far-reaching network—none of them could get any info on her.*

HY: That's because your people don't know these people. They won't . . . ever. Anyway, she made contact with me through them while we were at the center in Kaikoura. When I found out she was okay, the relief I felt made me realize I had been basically holding my breath since our conversation. I tend to live in a state of being on guard, but the amount of tension I had been holding in my body was next level. I guess it had been slowly building—kind of like the frog in the pot that slowly comes to a boil—and I had just grown accustomed to being on high alert. Anyway, I wasn't sure what to do at first. I definitely didn't know who to trust. For all I knew, it could have been a trap. I couldn't even tell Abe about it until I had time to game out all of the possible repercussions of pursuing this.

*What did they want from you? You weren't really in a position to do anything for her.*

HY: I'm not sure they knew exactly what they wanted. They just believed if anyone could help her—figure out what the hell was really going on and what to do about it—it would be me.

*Sheesh. No pressure there. .*

HY: No kidding. I mean, it was a nice little boost to my ego, but that crash-landed about the time that Lucas was attacked and I saw just how powerless I was.

*That was a really tough situation. I felt for the guy.*

HY: Me too. I'm not sure how he's going to come out after all of this. I definitely think going back in was a mistake, but it's not my call. Above all, he needed to do whatever made him feel safest for now. Time will tell.

*So, what are you hearing, seeing, thinking?*

HY: Well, word from the grapevine is that a tidal wave of blowback is coming.

*Are you talking about the rumored split? Abe and I discussed that a little.*

HY: Oh, it's not a rumor. There is a massive groundswell on both sides. No one is happy with the state of affairs. The one thing they agree on is that Marshall has to go because she completely botched the handling of our return and everything that has happened since. But that's where the unity ends. They are about as far apart as you can get on how to go about making that happen and what comes next.

*Are we talking coup d'etat?*

HY: It could come to that. Her term is almost over, so it might just happen at the polls, but some aren't willing to wait that long, and they don't trust the normal channels for removal.

*That sounds ominous.*

HY: I don't mean to overdramatize things, but the direction this is heading has been a long time coming.

*So you really do think a split is possible?*

HY: Not just possible . . . imminent. There are camps on both sides running the scenarios for what that looks like and how to do it in a way that minimizes the casualties for the regular people. The elites and the politicians be damned.

*What does that mean?*

HY: You might call it an informal Constitutional Convention, just not with the existing leadership involved.

*Whoa! Seriously? It's gone that far?*

HY: It would seem so. Still, that's no guarantee this will get beyond a cerebral exercise. It remains to be seen. I have a feeling that's why Marshall set her sights on me.

*Okay. You're going to have to clarify that.*

HY: I guess I skipped a few steps. Backing up . . . Around the time that I was starting to get my brain around everything that had happened, and was forming an inkling of an idea of what I might be able to do about any of it, I was called into the Center administrator's office. When I got there, Marshall was sitting behind the desk.

*That must have been quite a surprise.*

HY: Definitely unexpected. She cut right to the chase.

*Isn't that a refreshing change.*

HY: Honestly, I think that's the kind of woman she really is. All of the evasiveness and feet dragging we experienced initially was more from truly not knowing what to do than some game she was playing. I don't think she was giving us the runaround as a way of some political maneuvering. She really just couldn't tell her ass from a hole in the ground at the time. It was probably an incredibly rare moment of vulnerability for her.

*That's being pretty generous, considering.*

HY: You know, we're all human and trying to figure this out as we go. At any rate she dove right in, telling me why she was there and what she wanted. And, to be clear, even though she didn't mess around, I don't, for one second, think she was playing it straight with me. But she made me an offer and I agreed to her terms, in part because it wasn't exactly presented as optional. Also, it seemed to be the opening we needed to get a little leverage. After we shook hands and she slipped away, I used my same channels to get a message to Statham about what was unfolding.

*Did anyone else know she had visited you?*

HY: If they did, they weren't letting on. Incidentally . . . or maybe it's not incidental at all. It could be very relevant. Marshall wasn't the only bigwig who made a stealthy drop-in at the Center.

*Oh?*

HY: I didn't see her, but, apparently, the day before, Pearce got a visit from the president of Africa.

*Really? Do you think Marshall knew about this?*

HY: Wouldn't be surprised. The timing of her visit is suspect.

*So, what did she want?*

HY: She made a pitch to him.

*Like what Marshall did with you?*

HY: Sort of, but not exactly. She had heard about his attempt to escape, so she guessed he would be ripe for the picking. She told him she could arrange for him to change his citizenship and become her consort. She offered him way more for his "services" than the Center on the condition that he provide his semen to her region exclusively. I think she is hoping to preserve some racial integrity or something.

*I don't even know where to begin with all the ways that is just wrong. Racial considerations, notwithstanding.*

HY: Won't get any argument from me.

*Well, what did he do?*

HY: He's leaving . . . actually, already left . . . defecting, I guess you could say. They knew they couldn't hold us there against our will without lighting a short fuse to a really big pile of dynamite. So he is going off to literally be the father of a nation.

*Unbelievable! That means the numbers at the Center are dwindling.*

HY: That's why they were so relieved Lucas came back. He's being treated like a king there.

*How many are left?*

HY: Um, let's see. We had eighteen to begin with, and then we lost Harris in the abduction.

*Such a pointless loss.*

HY: Completely unnecessary. But, even in death, they still managed to make use of him.

*You don't mean . . .*

HY: I wish I could say it wasn't true. He may not be in the head count at the Center, but he is still adding to the sperm count. Anyway, so, technically, we were down to seventeen. After the summit, when they gave us the contract, we lost Abe, Kamil, and the Flemming kid. That brought us down to fourteen. Now that Pearce is gone, and I'm at loose ends, they have twelve there. If you count what they collected from Harris and froze in the bank, they have thirteen.

*How is this a real conversation we are having? How are we in this state of affairs?*

HY: You are asking the wrong person. Remember? I was off in some vortex for the last four decades. You're what? Around forty?

*Yeah, this year.*

HY: Interesting. My celibacy streak is about as old as you are. I guess the last time I had to think about any of this was probably around the time your parents were planning for you.

*That's assuming they planned.*

HY: Fair enough. Anyway, they can't afford to lose any more guys, but they will be okay with what they have for now. But this is just the quick-fix part of the plan. Obviously, the primary focus is on finding a cure. I hear there may be some good news coming in that regard soon.

*Already?*

HY: I wouldn't go telling anyone that yet and getting hopes up. But having our DNA to study has helped them in making significant headway pretty rapidly. It remains to be seen, but those in the know seem pretty excited.

*That would be great, and very welcome, news.*

HY: It would. I don't think it's going to stem the tide of the revolution coming in the Americas though.

*So let's go back to Marshall's offer. You said what Africa offered Pearce was similar, but not quite the same.*

HY: Yeah, Marshall said she wanted me to come and be a sort of goodwill ambassador—someone who could put on a brave face, speak to the country, calm their fears, that sort of thing—and represent the interests of the crew going forward as they rolled out this repopulation initiative.

*And she picked you for that? Has she met you?*

HY: Yeah, I know. Not the most logical choice, huh?

*Although you do have the whole national hero thing going for you—that has to bring some good PR with it.*

HY: I don't think it's going to have the effect she is hoping for.

*Why is that?*

HY: Like I said, there's a lot of toothpaste already out of the tube. The trust has been broken and I don't know of anything I can say or do to fix that for her. I can't say I agree with what they are proposing. There has been nonstop global turmoil for so long, I don't think anyone knows what end is up anymore. All of this feels very reactionary and had not been considered well. But I also know people are gonna do what they're gonna do.

*That's true. But I think I'm missing something. So you were on your way to the White House at the request of President Marshall. How did you end up hiding out with Statham?*

HY: Yeah, so I agreed to meet with Marshall in DC to weigh in on some policy discussions and show my face at a presser, where she would bring everyone up to speed on the state of things.

*I saw that. What were your thoughts on how it went?*

HY: From her perspective it went well, and on the way back to the White House, she was already planning for other ways to use me. Here's the thing. I knew basically what I was getting myself into, so it didn't surprise me that she wanted to get her money's worth. I just didn't anticipate feeling so dirty from it. I guess I thought I could justify it if it made some difference. But it didn't move the needle. After that dog and pony show, I heard from Statham through the back channels again. I still am in awe of the network they have . . . to be able to reach me in the middle of the lion's den! Anyway, she got word to me that I didn't want to be in the blast zone around Marshall and needed to distance myself.

*That sounds like a threat.*

HY: If Secret Service had caught wind of it, it could have gotten bad. But she wasn't talking about actual physical violence . . . at least I don't think she was then. She meant political fallout. She didn't want me caught up in that and seen as Marshall's shill. None of it was sitting well with me anyway, so I agreed to let them help with an extraction.

*Haven't you had enough of that sort of thing?*

HY: More than enough for many lifetimes, my friend. But I hoped this would be the last time.

*How did they pull it off? Weren't you under guard by . . . the army or something?*

HY: Not exactly. I'm sure I was being watched really closely, but they didn't want to give the appearance that I was a prisoner, so everything was from a distance. I had a bodyguard for my "protection," but that person was swapped out for someone else the next day. The new guard was one of Statham's people.

*Boy, you weren't kidding about that network.*

HY: Yep. Subversives operate in mysterious ways. So, that evening, it was "strongly suggested" to me that I request an evening alone to decompress from another full day of meetings on the Hill. Good cover, and, honestly, I probably would have asked for that anyway. I hate all of that bureaucratic madness. About an hour after dinner my bodyguard knocked on my door and she was joined by two others, who threw some tactical gear at me and told me to suit up. Within fifteen minutes we were slipping down a back staircase into an underground tunnel away from 1600 and resurfaced about ten minutes later near the Lincoln Memorial. From there I was taken to a safe house, where Statham was waiting for me, and we've basically been on the move ever since.

*Incredible. So, what's the plan now?*

HY: I'm going back in.

*What? Why? After all they went through to get you out?*

HY: They need me inside. Things are shifting rapidly and they want to allay any suspicions so they don't reveal their hand too soon.

*How are you going to explain your absence?*

HY: Play the victim. Someone seized the opportunity of my being away from the center to steal me again.

*I guess that could work. If it happened once, it could happen again. You all are pretty hot commodities.*

HY: It would seem so.

*Still, I would be really careful. She could be onto you already and be playing dumb.*

HY: I'm sure there's a chance of that, but she suffers from the fatal flaw of all evil geniuses.

*Which is?*

HY: Being ultimately self-serving. The political game wasn't the real reason she wanted me there anyway. That was just the pretense.

*So that's not why you went? What was the reason?*

HY: Well, I think she did want me in her administration to keep the natives from getting restless. That much was legit. But that only served her interests so far as keeping her afloat through the end of her term and salvaging her reputation.

*So, what did she want? Why would she take you back without question?*

HY: For the same reason all of us guys were at the Center to begin with. She was just taking advantage of her position of authority to skip the line. She wanted her own private supplier to help her produce a legacy.

*I'm going to take a wild guess and say you don't mean her legacy as president.*

HY: You're a clever one, aren't you? Of course not. She knows the handwriting is on the wall with that one. This is about her personal legacy, about not being alone at the end of her life.

*You've got to be kidding me. It just doesn't stop with her. I know a few activists who would have a field day with this information.*

HY: Well, you can't tell them.

*Why not? The public deserves to know what an unscrupulous . . .*

HY: Look, they will know soon enough. Right now it is to my . . . our . . . strategic advantage to not make waves.

*I can't believe I'm hearing you, of all people, say this.*

HY: I'm just being a pragmatist. There is a lot you don't know . . . that the whole world doesn't know . . . that is happening behind the scenes. I'm not talking about the Illuminati or cabal conspiracy theories.

*The what?*

HY: Never mind. Something from the past. My point is, there are things in play that make it a really smart move for us to have someone on the inside who sees through their bullshit.

*So you're just going to let her use you?*

HY: For now.

*And you're going to give her what she wants? A . . . legacy?*

HY: Hell, I don't know about that. Nature has a whole lot to say in that regard, but I will be giving her something else she wants in the meantime.

*What's that?*

HY: A hero she can parade in front of cameras so she can pretend she is doing something to make everyone feel safe and hopeful again. She may know her fate is sealed, but she still has to keep up appearances. And, honestly, we need the façade to remain in place a little longer if we are going to dig ourselves out of this hole.

*I don't know. It sounds an awful lot like compromising your integrity. Sleeping with the enemy.*

HY: Hey, she's an attractive woman, and it's been way too long.

*What is wrong with you? This doesn't sound like the Hunter I've come to know. Children aren't pawns.*

HY: I was kidding. I'm not really that cynical, but you seem to be taking this really personally. What's up?

*Nothing . . . never mind . . . I mean, I just . . . You have been a truth-to-power, fight-for-the-underdog kind of guy all along. How are you giving in so easily?*

HY: Well, first . . . I'm not. I am using an opportunity I have to work this from a different angle. It's about seeing the whole landscape. I've finally learned something Abe has been trying to get me to see for a long time—that there's more than one way to skin a cat. And second, I am still a truth-to-power kind of guy, but I see the wisdom in picking my battles. You know, you are really passionate in your righteous indignation. I can respect that. It kind of reminds me of . . . well . . . me.

*It's funny you mention that . . .*

*Final Note:*

*You have likely guessed, this is by no means the end of the story. It is, however, the end of the information I have collected to date. I hope to follow up with each of the crew members when the dust settles. Circumstances have devolved in such a way that the previous agreement to withhold the information from these interviews is no longer possible. I am releasing this content now because it is needed.*

*Though we have seen a great deal of progress around the population recovery, we are seeing a significant regression in terms of domestic (American) and global politics. The rift over what has to be done to save the human race and the compromises required to get it done is dividing this country along those old red and blue party lines. They had essentially dissolved during my lifetime but have seen a resurgence to such a degree that we are looking at the country becoming segregated into red zones and blue zones—mostly rural vs. urban—with state lines being redrawn and the rumored writing of two new constitutions. In light of what we've seen recently, "unprecedented" is becoming an overused word, and yet still relevant.*

*But, as I mentioned, there is progress. As of this writing, there are still twelve members of the crew at the Center in Kaikoura, New Zealand. They are nearing their first year of service there. The repopulation program has resulted in nearly 400,000 pregnancies, with the first children born approximately two months ago, and a steady flow of new births weekly since. Initial testing indicates the males being born show no signs of the genetic abnormality, though their reproductive capabilities won't be effectively determined for years. You may be wondering about how this will work when they are of age to begin reproducing on their own. The plan put into place provided for a percentage of the women of childbearing age to agree to be inseminated with female embryos fertilized by the "untainted" sperm so there would be female children of the same age who also had not been contaminated by the plague. So far, so good. It seems to be unfolding according to the projections. I suppose we have all agreed to simply turn a blind eye to the unpalatable aspects of trying to repopulate the earth with such a small group of people coming from the same gene pool.*

*There is word of a cure, though it has not been tested in humans yet, and replication of it holds some challenges. However, there is promise of something forthcoming within the next year—just in time for the expiration of the crew contracts, it would seem. I'm praying to whatever god might be listening that this solution manifests soon.*

*Those who chose not to stay at the center have reintegrated into society, though the transition has been quite bumpy. Abe and Sarah have settled in Vancouver, British Columbia . . . and much to their surprise, they are expecting a child in a few months. I guess miracles really do happen, at least for this crew. They were not trying, but that's usually when these surprises happen. I am proof of that.*

*Sean and Natalie Flemming went back to the Seattle area, where they grew up. They remain close to Abe and Sarah and visit often. Kamil lives with his oldest daughter and her family in El Paso, Texas. Pearce Johnson found his life in South Africa to be a far cry from the life he was expecting. Yes, he is getting the royal treatment, but he is finding it isn't worth the sacrifices in terms of his personal freedom. However, he is stuck for now. The remainder of the crew has begun rebuilding their lives, most of them out of the public eye, some with their remaining family members, some on their own.*

*A national memorial service for Sonja Halverson was one of the first things Hunter pushed through in his new role in the Marshall administration, and he managed to get an annual day honoring her put on the calendar as well.*

*As for Lydia Statham, she continues to work covertly, pulling strings behind the curtain to bring full disclosure as the Marshall tenure winds down and the country heads in a new direction . . . actually two directions. There are very important decisions on the ballot come November. I will continue to provide updates as the ground beneath our feet continues to shift.*

*Now, I am sure you are curious about my story as well. While I am not the focus of this work, I will answer a couple of questions. My father had a brief affair with my mother right before he was called away on a mission. She did not discover she was pregnant until he was gone and out of reach. He was lost to us in the line of duty, and he never knew I existed. All of that changed about a year ago, and now we are trying to navigate this unexpected relationship. There is nothing more to say about it at this point, though our story is just getting started.*

*Thank you for your support of our efforts and your interest in the truth.*

*—Jacob Young*

# ACKNOWLEDGEMENTS

This story has been taking shape in my mind for many years, and when we finally began working on it in 2018, I had no idea how relevant it would become. It has been incredible to see so much of this play out in real life. I hope those who read it will take away some insight that is useful for this time.

I would like to thank my family for their support and would like to thank my sisters, Toni and Mary, as well as Tim and Myriah Garvey, Grace Garvey, Paul and Natalie Botes, Pat McGinley, and John Highsmith for being early readers and offering helpful comments. I would also like to thank Chad Jones and Angela Moscheo Benson for consulting on various components of the story.

Finally, I would like to thank Brian and Grace McLaren for introducing me to Cara Highsmith and helping me take a big step forward in bringing the dream of writing this story to fruition.